"I want to fin[...]

Kelly licked her lips nervously. "But we're not the same people anymore."

"Maybe not, but we're both still attracted to each other, and that's not about to go away." Diamere pulled her closer. "Agree to have dinner with me."

Kelly had to tilt her head to meet his eyes. Before she could protest, Diamere brought his lips down against hers, his tongue effortlessly opening her mouth to his, and then she felt it. Passion.

And when his tongue slid across hers, she heard a moan. It took her a second before she realized it had come from her. She brought her arms around his neck and locked her fingers and leaned in closer. The blood surged through her veins, lowering her resistance, making her forget all the reasons kissing him again was wrong.

None of that mattered right now. His lips were hot and urgent and so damn irresistible. This was what she had been longing for for so many years. His taste. His smell. The feel of his body next to hers.

As the kiss deepened, all Kelly could think about were her wants and desires, and right now she wanted him desperately. The feel of his mouth on hers, his tongue dancing with hers, his body pressing against hers was all too much. She wanted him so badly her body was humming with a need she had never felt before.

Books by Angie Daniels

Kimani Romance

The Second Time Around
The Playboy's Proposition
The Player's Proposal
For You I Do
Before I Let You Go

ANGIE DANIELS

is an award-winning author of romance and fiction. A chronic daydreamer, she knew early in life that someday she wanted to create page turning stories of love and adventure. Born in Chicago, Angie has spent the past twenty years residing in and around Missouri and considers the state her home. Angie holds a master's degree in human resource management. For more information you can visit her Web site at www.angiedaniels.com.

BEFORE
I Let You Go

ANGIE DANIELS

KIMANI
ROMANCE

KIMANI PRESS™

Recycling programs
for this product may
not exist in your area.

ISBN-13: 978-0-373-86154-5

BEFORE I LET YOU GO

www.kimanipress.com

Printed in U.S.A.

Dear Reader,

Welcome back to Sheraton Beach!

I truly miss living in Delaware, with its beautiful oceanfront views and the warm sand between my toes. It's the reason I have invited you back so often to spend time visiting the lovely state with the Beaumonts.

A number of readers have asked, and I hate to break it to you, but Sheraton Beach is a fictional town I created. However, there are several places just as beautiful along the coast of Delaware if you're looking for a sunny getaway.

I truly enjoyed writing the stories of Jabarie, Jace, Jaden and Bianca. Each of them realized—just by opening their eyes and hearts—that love had been standing right in front of them all along. Now it's Diamere's turn to find true love.

To all the fans of the Beaumonts, I hope this last book in the series is everything you've been waiting for. So kick back and enjoy the sun!

Happy reading,

Angie Daniels

Chapter 1

Music bumping. Heads bobbing. Kellis Saunders couldn't help but feel the rush of excitement as she stepped into the hottest new nightclub in central Philadelphia—Ja'net.

She showed the doorman her driver's license and paid the cover charge, then hovered near the double doors while she waited for her sister-in-law.

"All right, let's go, Kelly," Essence said, with excitement bubbling in her voice as she moved up beside her.

Kelly took a look at the hundreds of people inside, and said, "Wow! You were right, Essence. This place is jumping."

The caramel beauty's sienna-brown eyes danced knowingly. "I told you," she answered over the thump of the music. "Mark brought me here last month and we had a great time." Once inside, Essence looked around, then signaled for Kelly to follow her up a small spiral staircase that took them to a long balcony.

Kelly had to do a double take when she spotted the lush, red velvet couches, round mahogany tables and private bar at the far left of the room. Essence flashed two VIP passes and they moved over to an empty couch close to a banister. Kelly took a seat and rubbed her hands across the fabric, loving the feel of velvet against her skin.

"Dang, this place is nice! Whoever owns it knows exactly what he's doing."

"I told you so."

Looking around, Kelly nodded in agreement. "Yes, you did, but you still haven't told me how you got us VIP passes."

Essence lowered her eyes to the crowded dance floor below and shrugged. "Your brother knows the owner."

Before Kelly could ask another question, a waitress came over and they each ordered a cosmopolitan.

Crossing her bare legs, Kelly glanced down at the white Deréon designer stilettos on her feet. She had complemented the daring shoes with a short, white spandex skirt and a fire-engine-red halter top that left her flat midriff bare and exposed. But looking around at the other women dressed in slamming outfits that had to have cost way more than she could ever afford on a teacher's salary, Kelly felt insecure about her choice.

"You look fabulous," Essence said.

Kelly grinned. Her sister-in-law always had a way of reading her mind. "Thanks. Although I must say, for someone with three children, you're the one that looks amazing."

"Thanks, girl." Essence was wearing a daring pink

strapless dress that plunged low in the back and hugged every curve imaginable. One could only hope to look that good after having children.

"Speaking of kids..." Essence began as she glanced down at the slender gold watch on her wrist. "I think I need to call your mom and see how Summer is doing." Before she could reach inside her small Coach purse for her phone, Kelly touched her arm, halting her.

"Girl, relax. They're fine. You know Mama has everything under control."

Essence hesitated for a moment before she finally relaxed her shoulders and nodded. "Yes, you're right."

Smiling, Kelly looked down at the three-carat diamond ring that glittered on her sister-in-law's finger, and felt a twinge of envy. Essence and Mark, Kelly's big brother, were the proud parents of three wonderful children. Tyler was eight, Chelsea was four, and Summer had just turned six months old. Kelly adored her nieces and nephew. Other than teaching her second-grade class, she enjoyed nothing as much as being an aunt.

While they waited for their drinks, she took a deep breath and told herself to relax. *I deserve a night out.* It had been a long week, getting ready for the upcoming school year, and she realized she needed some fun. Despite her initial opposition to being a third wheel, now she thought that hanging out with her brother and his wife could turn out to be fun.

Snapping her fingers, she sang along with Keyshia Cole and allowed her eyes to travel around the club. Everybody from executives to gold diggers had come out to party, and they were all dressed to impress. Below, to the far right of the main level, Kelly spotted someone that made her gasp. "Isn't that Donovan McNabb, of the Philadelphia Eagles?"

Essence followed the direction of her gaze and nodded. "Oh my goodness, it is! He is so good-looking."

Nodding, Kelly watched the NFL player, noting that he looked smaller in person. He was standing near the main bar talking to someone who looked vaguely familiar. Kelly furrowed her brow as she searched her mind, trying to recall where she had seen him before. *If only I could see his eyes.* To her disappointment, he never turned her way. Still, even from watching his profile, she felt a dizzying current race up her arms. The football star had since moved across the room, but he was of no interest to her. Instead, Kelly allowed her eyes to follow the handsome stranger around the club. *This is crazy,* she thought. The man had grabbed her attention and she couldn't stop looking at him. Her heart began to pound rapidly within her chest and Kelly started to wonder what in the world was wrong with her. She couldn't blame it on alcohol because she hadn't had a drink yet. And it wasn't like it had been a while since she'd noticed a gorgeous man—she'd seen two earlier while shopping in the mall. Both had stopped to ask for her phone number, and been politely turned down. After a terrible breakup, Kellis wasn't interested in dating, and rarely gave a man a second thought. Yet as she continued to stare at the floor below, she couldn't recall the last time she had felt this drawn to a man. There was something about him because, even from a distance, his mere presence carried a strong sense of masculine power.

Tilting her head, she studied the chiseled lines of his profile, admiring his prominent nose and high

cheekbones. Maybe it was his deep coffee complexion—
she always had a thing for dark men. No, it was something else. Maybe it was his massive chest or that he
was well over six feet tall. Kellis loved tilting her head
back to gaze up into a man's eyes.

The longer she stared at the handsome stranger, the
more puzzled she became. She couldn't put her finger
on it, but was certain the two of them had crossed paths
at some point in her life. The big questions were when
and where?

The waitress returned with their drinks, and
Kelly brushed her curiosity aside. She accepted the
cosmopolitan and insisted on paying for the first round
of drinks. Kelly reached into her purse and gave the
waitress enough to include a tip. She thanked them, and
as soon as she moved to the next table, Kelly brought the
drink to her lips and nodded. "Mmm, there's nothing
better than a nice club with good music and wonderful
drinks!"

"Mark's thoughts exactly," Essence said, then glanced
down at her watch again, frowning slightly. "I wonder
what's taking him so long?"

They had left him standing out in the parking lot
talking to a guy he hadn't seen in years. "I'm sure he's
around somewhere. You know my brother. He always
seems to know everybody." Pausing with the martini
glass halfway to her lips, Kelly looked down at the floor
again and felt a sting of disappointment upon discovering
her mystery man was no longer there. It was probably for
the best, because given the way he had made her skin
tingle, there was no telling what she might be willing
to do if he had asked for her number. One thing was for
sure, she definitely wouldn't have turned him down.

The music changed to a funky new Beyoncé tune. Kelly lowered her drink to the coffee table, then hopped out of her seat. While holding on to the rail, she moved to the beat. "Hey! That's my jam."

Essence also jumped to her feet and the two of them rocked to the thump of the music. Down below, the dance floor was packed, and others were climbing out of their seats, trying to push their way through the crowd. The two women waved their hands in the air and then started doing the bump. Kelly was dancing and laughing so hard she couldn't remember the last time she'd had this much fun.

"Damn, girl! Where's your man at?"

The two women swung around and Kelly playfully rolled her eyes at her brother. "Don't have one. Don't want one."

Mark gave her a dismissive wave. "I wasn't talking to you. I was talking to that sexy female standing beside you."

Essence sucked her teeth and played along. "My man will be here shortly, and he's really jealous, so you better get to stepping before he arrives."

"Well, in that case, let's give him something to be pissed off about." Mark moved up beside his wife and snaked a possessive arm around her waist. Leaning forward, he pressed his lips against hers in a long, sensual kiss. Kelly smiled with envy as she watched the two. The couple had been married almost seven years after the former United States Air Force captain returned home on leave to discover the one night he'd spent with Essence had produced a son. With relentless determination, he'd pursued the fourth-grade schoolteacher until Essence accepted his offer to spend their lives together. After a boating accident caused limited mobility in his left hand, Mark had retired from the military, and he and his family had returned to Wilmington, Delaware.

After one final kiss, Mark released his wife, then focused his attention on his little sister. "I see you're having a good time."

Kelly nodded. "Yes, coming out tonight was just what I needed. I love this place. It's classy and vibrant. Thanks, big brother, this is great."

"You're welcome."

She gave him a big squeeze, then lowered herself back into her seat again. "And thank you for the VIP passes. Essence said the owner's a friend of yours."

A mischievous smile touched Mark's lips. "Yes, as a matter of fact he is, and here he comes now."

Kelly followed the direction of his gaze toward the spiral staircase, and her breath caught in her throat when she noticed it was the handsome stranger she had been watching earlier. He started in their direction. Just as before, her heart began to pound heavily as her eyes scanned him from his wingtip shoes to his smooth dark face. When she reached his large chocolate eyes, her stomach clenched with recognition.

Oh.

My.

Goodness.

She knew him. She knew him well.

As Kelly took a deep breath, she looked over at her brother and at Essence, who were both staring down at the dance floor, avoiding eye contact. The knowing looks on their faces told her tonight had been a setup.

"Hello, Kellis."

Her birth name coming from his full sensual lips was

a whisper so soft it felt like a caress, and almost made her whimper. Tilting her head, Kelly stared up at the man she had fallen in love with when she was barely a teenager.

Diamere Redmond.

Her pulse raced as he looped an arm around her waist and hugged her close. With his hard body against her, she felt her head begin to spin, and her own body came wildly alive. And all from a simple hug. Only, there was nothing simple about it, or the man holding her.

Diamere finally released her and for several seconds Kelly was speechless, too in shock to form any kind of coherent response. Instead, she gazed up into the chocolate depths of his eyes until she found her breath. "Hi," she began, stopping to clear the frog from her throat. "I didn't know you were back on the East Coast."

"Been back almost a year now," he replied, grinning broadly.

A whole year and no one told me, she thought. She glanced out of the corner of her eyes at Mark and pursed her lips with disapproval.

She looked back once again and met the intense gaze of Diamere, who was standing so close Kelly could smell the succulent woody scent of his cologne. It was a familiar smell that made her sway toward him, longing to rest her cheek on his chest and simply inhale. It was as if they were the only two people standing there as she became lost admiring him. A few lines had developed in the corners of his eyes, which were deep, dark and mysterious, reminding her of a dark winter night. The firmness of his jaw made his face more angular than she remembered. His coffee-colored features were still disturbingly handsome. The shape of his luscious mouth was and always would be a turn-on, and he still had those sexy dimples he used to flash at her so often. Gone were his thick curls, replaced by a short, even haircut.

"I thought you were teaching in Texas." Diamere's deep voice broke into her trip down memory lane.

"I was. But I missed Wilmington," she said, barely audible above the beat of the music. For so long she had imagined seeing him again. She'd thought she would be prepared, but everything she had practiced, everything she had planned to say, was gone. Her mind had drawn a blank. Instead, all she could do was stare.

I must be dreaming.

Kelly blinked once, then twice, but Diamere was still there standing right before her, looking better than any man had a right to look. And for that reason she couldn't tear her eyes away from him no matter how hard she tried. All she could do was stand there as she remembered that this was the man she had once loved to distraction. The same man she dreamed would be the father of her children. The man to whom she'd vowed to give her virginity.

"You okay?" she heard him ask.

Kelly blinked twice more, then cleared her throat. Damn, she was pathetic. *You're making a fool of yourself.* The last thing she wanted was for Diamere to think she had been pining over him all these years. Swallowing sharply, she pulled herself together. "I'm fine. Just a little surprised to see you." A smile curled her lips as she met his grin. "I hear you own this club?"

He shifted his weight to his other foot as he spoke. "Not that I'm trying to brag, but I actually own *three* nightclubs."

A big smile crinkled her eyes. "Three? Dang! You're doing big things."

Diamere held her gaze as he replied, "Just trying to get paid."

She dragged her gaze away from him long enough to glance around the room in admiration. But Diamere had such beautiful eyes they were like a magnet, so looking away wasn't easy. "Well, I'd say you're definitely doing that."

Taking another deep breath, Kelly groaned inwardly as her head suddenly cleared long enough for her to remember. Diamere was wearing Armani cologne. He'd had it on the last time they were together, seven years ago. She'd know that fragrance anywhere. Only on Diamere it blended with his natural scent and smelled as if the designer had created it specifically for him.

With a will of its own, her mind traveled back to a time when Diamere had held her tightly in his arms and she hadn't a worry in the world. All she had cared about was that exact moment and the man whose arms engulfed her like a warm blanket.

"Why don't we all move over to my table in the corner?" Diamere suggested, in a voice so soft and seductive you would have thought he'd asked her to go home to his bed.

Kelly nodded, and he linked his arm around hers as he escorted her to his private table. As soon as he touched her, heat radiated from his body, causing her skin to tingle. Walking beside him, she barely felt her feet on the ground. She sighed with relief when she finally sank onto the upholstered chair beside his, glad that he'd released her. With him so close, brushing up against her, Kelly wasn't sure how much longer she would have managed to keep her legs from giving out.

Diamere was just about to take a seat when his eyes traveled over to the bar in the far corner, and he frowned. "Excuse me. One of my bartenders is requesting my assistance."

As soon as he was gone, Kelly glared across the table at her brother and Essence. "How come neither of you told me Diamere was back in town, not to mention the fact that he owns this club?"

Mark chuckled loudly and boisterously, the way he always did when he'd been found out by his younger sister, while Essence looked guilty.

"Sorry, Kelly. I was afraid if you knew he owned the club you wouldn't have come," she confessed.

"Yes, I would have," Kellis replied defensively.

"No, you wouldn't," Mark joined in.

Mark was right. She wouldn't have. She had spent too many years hoping and praying that Diamere would stop treating her like a child and notice her for the beautiful woman she was. But by the time he had, he'd ended up marrying his baby's mama. Now Kellis was over him, and she didn't want him to think for a moment she was still interested.

"Why wouldn't I come? Diamere and I have never been anything but friends," she said with a defiant tilt of her chin.

Essence gave her a look that said she knew better.

Mark rose from his chair. "This is one conversation I don't want to be a part of. I'm going to go get another beer. Either of you want something?"

Essence looked up at her husband adoringly. "Yes. Baby, can you get me another cosmopolitan?"

"Me, too," Kelly replied. She had a feeling she was going to be drinking quite a few this evening.

She looked over at the bar, where Diamere was standing. The man had a stance that reeked of confidence and she wasn't the only one who noticed. She watched a voluptuous woman dressed in spandex pants and a blouse that revealed way too much cleavage approach him. The way she was leaning toward him suggested she was trying to make her presence known. Jealousy curled inside Kelly, taking her by surprise. What was going on? She had never been the jealous type before, yet there was something about Diamere enjoying this woman's attention that worked on her nerves.

Essence crossed her arms. "He looks good, doesn't he?"

Kelly blinked upon realizing her friend had spoken. It hadn't occurred to her that she'd been sitting there staring at him. Kelly turned in her seat and said, "I can't believe you didn't tell me he was back!"

"I didn't think it was a good idea. But after the way I see you looking at him tonight…" She allowed her voice to trail off. "Now I'm not so sure."

Kelly took a deep breath and swallowed. At one time Diamere had meant the world to her. But now she was at a different point in her life.

"Diamere and I will always be friends and that will never change. He has always been like a big brother."

Essence snorted rudely. "Big brother? Well, let me tell you something. That's not the way you look at a big brother."

Kelly glanced in Diamere's direction and noticed the woman leaving with her lips twisted in disappointment. *Good for her.*

"You're drooling again."

Frowning, she turned to Essence. "You should know me better than that. I don't drool over married men."

Essence's brow bunched with a puzzled look. "Married? Oh, no! Mark didn't tell you?"

It was now Kelly's turned to be confused. "Tell me what?"

"Diamere's been divorced for almost a year."

"What?" Essence couldn't possibly have said what she thought she had. "He's not with Ryan?"

Essence gave her a weak smile. "Nope."

Covering her mouth with one hand, Kelly closed her eyes and tried to compose herself. She didn't realize how much her heart was pounding until she turned her head and found Diamere staring across the room at her. Instantly, a shiver of desire tore through her, and she could feel her pulse quicken. *He's single.* After all those years of hoping and wishing, was it possible to finally—

Nope. She wasn't even going to go there. Yet she couldn't stop herself from watching him with fascination as he helped out behind the bar. It wasn't long before he was laughing, his deep robust voice traveling over to her table.

The years had been good to him. Diamere was thicker, wider than she remembered. Shoulders broader. Chest massive. It was definitely a good thing. She always had a thing for a man with a rugged build. Feeling someone pinching her under the table, she flinched and snapped her head toward her friend.

"You're still drooling," Essence said, and started laughing.

Frowning, Kelly wiped her mouth, just to make

sure she wasn't serious, then reached for her drink and finished it. If Essence noticed her staring, that meant her attraction for Diamere was way too obvious—not a good idea. The last thing she wanted was for Diamere to think she was interested in him…again.

Kelly found herself looking in his direction once more and realized she needed something, anything, to break the attraction she was feeling for him. Trying to regain control of herself, she forced her eyes away. There was no way she was falling for him again, she decided with a stubborn frown. She had already wasted enough years waiting, hoping that someday Diamere would notice she was all grown up. And when he'd married another woman, it had been like a kick in the gut. Still, it was exactly what Kelly had needed to force her to finally get over her schoolgirl crush and realize she and Diamere could never be. Even though he was single now, nothing else had changed as far as she was concerned.

She remembered what she'd learned over the years. A man who got too deep under a woman's skin could ultimately become her downfall, and Kelly wasn't about to let that happen. Besides, she needed to focus on completing her master's degree and the upcoming school year, not Diamere.

But as she stared across at his handsome face and found him looking back, Kelly realized that staying away from Diamere Redmond was going to be easier said than done.

Chapter 2

Diamere had been watching Kelly since she first stepped into Ja'net. The second he spotted her, his libido had kicked into gear. Even now he couldn't take his eyes off of her. Especially not with her dressed in a red tube top that dipped seductively low on her chest. He loved her new hairstyle. Gone were the short, natural curls and in their place was straight, shoulder-length dark brown hair combed back from her face. The style emphasized her luminous eyes, voluptuous mouth and high cheekbones.

That wasn't the only thing that had changed. Sure, it had been almost seven years since he'd last seen her, but even then she had always struck him as expressive and confident. But now she seemed even more poised and elegant than ever before. And of course there were her eyes. Large, cinnamon and round with a mesmerizing quality he'd never noticed before.

Diamere had met Mark when Kelly was in junior high. Back then he'd never thought of her as anything but a little sister. Until one night when everything changed. It was the year Mark returned home after a deployment to Germany, the very same year he discovered that, during his absence, Essence had given birth to his son. It was Christmas, and Mark had brought Essence home to meet the family. The memory of that evening would be forever etched in Diamere's mind.

From the moment Kelly stepped into the room, the very air he'd been breathing seemed to get snatched right from his lungs as he stared at her. And the second his eyes perused her shapely body, sensations hit him with the force of a tornado.

And now? Now his pulse was racing and blood was flowing hot through his veins. From the instant he'd first gazed into the eyes of the girl who had transformed into an amazing woman, he had felt an instant jolt identical to the one he was experiencing now.

Diamere knew he'd had a reputation for being a ladies' man, and back then there had been other women. But it was his best friend's little sister who had captivated his attention that holiday season. Kelly was different from the women he typically dated. He preferred them tall and high maintenance, while at five foot three, Kelly fit perfectly under his chin. She was small but had plenty of tantalizing curves.

A waitress standing at the end of the bar called for a Heineken beer, drawing Diamere's attention. He reached into a cooler and slid one across the bar, then returned his attention to the beauty sitting at his private table. They had some unfinished business.

Seven years ago he had been ready to give her his heart when Ryan had announced she was pregnant with twins. A muscle in his cheek twitched at the thought of the last several years. He had done everything he could to provide for his wife and what he thought were his children. It wasn't until Nichole fell from a jungle gym and was rushed to the hospital that he discovered his daughter had a rare blood type that belonged to neither him nor his wife. When he confronted Ryan, she'd finally confessed that not only were the twins not his, but she had started dating their real father again.

Theirs was a bitter divorce. Ryan took everything, yet nothing hurt Diamere more than losing his girls. Afterward he'd vowed never to let a woman get that close to him again. Over the last six months he had dated occasionally, but none of the women stirred him the way Kelly Saunders had done before, and was doing now. This was the first woman to arouse more than just his sexual desires since his divorce.

Standing behind the bar, Diamere turned and looked over at the table. His gaze swept across her face again, and he found himself focusing on those succulent lips as memories of the hottest kiss he'd ever experienced flooded back into his mind. It had happened with Kelly, and now, seeing her again, he knew once was not enough.

A part of him was intrigued by what he was feeling, while on the other hand he felt that maybe it was best to leave well enough alone. He had learned the hard way to stay clear of love. It had been a painful lesson.

Ryan had ripped his heart from his chest because he'd lowered his guard and given himself to her completely. And because of her he was no longer interested in commitment. Not now. Maybe not ever. Once burned was more than he could deal with. But that didn't mean he and Kelly couldn't spend time together, enjoying each other's company.

Diamere couldn't retract the smile that claimed his lips. He knew everything happened for a reason. And as far as he was concerned it was time he did something about the deep stab of desire that attacked him each and every time he looked at Kelly.

Kelly saw Diamere and Mark coming her way. Diamere's sensuous smile caused a sweet craving to invade her body. He wore dark slacks and a crisp white shirt that defined his broad shoulders, yet he still managed to look the part of successful businessman. And that made for one extremely sexy and dangerous man.

"Drinks are on me," he said, and lowered another cosmopolitan onto the table in front of her.

"Thanks."

Diamere took the seat across from Kelly, where she had no choice but to look his way. Their eyes collided several times before she swung on the seat and stared off at the crowd below.

"How have you been?"

At first Kelly pretended she didn't hear his question, then turned her head. "Oh, I'm sorry, did you say something?"

He smirked, flashing those deep dimples. "I asked how the last few years have been treating you."

She reached for her drink before meeting his eyes,

where she recognized genuine interest. It made her wonder if maybe Mark had told Diamere more than she cared for him to know. Leaning across the table so he could hear her over the thump of the music, she said, "I can't complain. I'm back teaching at Baer Elementary School with Essence."

"That's great," Diamere replied, then brought a glass of cognac to his lips.

She nodded. "I got lucky. The teacher they had gave birth to her first child in June and decided not to return. That opened the door for me to come back," she said between sips. "Other than that I am a thesis away from a master's in elementary education."

"That's wonderful." Diamere looked truly impressed. "I always knew you would be great at whatever path you chose."

For some reason the compliment made her feel even more nervous, so she lifted her glass and, instead of sipping, drained it in one gulp.

Diamere gave her an amused look. "You ready for another?"

Kelly had a feeling she was going to need quite a few if she was to get through tonight. "Sure. I don't get out much. Tonight, I'm planning to live a little."

"Or a lot," she heard Essence mumble under her breath.

Kelly gave her friend a warning look and was grateful that Essence decided to change the subject.

"Diamere, I'm loving your club, but you really need to rethink your waitresses' uniforms."

He glanced at Essence with a look of bewilderment. "What's wrong with their uniforms?"

"Yeah, what's wrong with them?" Mark chimed in,

but didn't miss the evil look Essence tossed his way. "Not that I'm looking. Sweetheart, the only woman I have eyes for is you."

Kelly studied the women moving across the floor dressed in short black shorts and formfitting white T-shirts with Ja'net spelled in big letters across their ample chests. She hadn't really paid their outfits any attention, but Essence did have a point. Dropping her head, Kelly tried to hide her laughter.

Diamere took a sip from his glass and shrugged. "It's a business move."

Disgust flashed across Essence's face. "It's a sexist move!"

Mark reached across the table for his wife's hand and squeezed it. "Man, forgive my wife."

Kelly couldn't resist giving her two cents. "She's right. This isn't a strip club."

"No, but sex sells," Diamere countered.

Essence crossed her arms defiantly. "We're not talking about sex. We're talking about your nightclub."

"Uh-oh. Watch out," Mark warned.

Turning her head, Essence glared at her husband and replied, "Stay out of this."

He held his hands up in surrender. "Hey, I can't just sit back and let the two of you gang up on my friend."

Kelly snorted. "Who's ganging up? Essence just asked a question. She wants to know why his waitresses are dressed like hoochies, and Diamere has yet to answer." For added measure she stuck her tongue out at her brother.

Diamere looked from Kelly to Essence, clearly amused. "Before you climb on your soapbox, I'll have you know I allowed the waitresses to come up with their own uniforms."

Essence's jaw dropped. "They picked that out?"

He nodded. "Yep. They're here to get paid, and if dressing like that increases their tips, who am I to object?"

Smiling, Essence leaned back in her seat. "Well, if the tips are that good, then maybe I should apply."

"What?" Mark cried in protest, before Diamere could say a word.

"You heard me." Essence stroked her husband's hand. "Sweetheart, you said you'd like to take a family vacation later this year. With the money I could make working here on Friday and Saturday nights, in *that* outfit, I'd have the money in no time."

"The hell you will!" Mark barked, then took an angry swig from his bottle of beer.

Kelly gave an eager nod. "It sounds like a wonderful idea. Sign me up, too."

Mark lowered his drink to the table with a thump. "The only place I want my wife on Friday and Saturday nights is at home in my arms." The music changed just then, to a new, slow beat. Mark rose and turned to Essence. "Come on, sweetheart, let's dance."

Eyes crinkled with laughter, she looked at Kelly and winked before taking her husband's proffered hand, then followed him to the small dance floor in the corner.

"Are those two always like that?" Diamere asked with an amused look.

Kelly nodded. "Pretty much."

The waitress returned with a tray of drinks. She lowered it onto the table, then left to help another customer. Diamere lifted one of the martini glasses and set it in front of Kelly. Suddenly at a loss for words, she reached for her drink and took a sip, grateful for the way the cold liquid soothed her dry throat.

"Care to dance?"

Kelly glanced over her shoulder at the couples holding each other intimately on the dance floor. Goodness, there was no way she could be that close to Diamere and maintain her composure.

He leaned forward. "I don't bite."

Tilting the glass, she took another sip, then rose from her seat. Kelly swung the strap of her small white Dooney & Bourke purse over her bare shoulder, then placed her hand in his. The moment she felt the heat of his hand, those familiar sensations began snaking up her arm. She gasped and looked up at Diamere. The intense expression in his eyes told her that he felt it, too. His strong fingers closed around hers and he led her to the dance floor. When she stepped into his embrace, she instantly felt his masculine warmth. As they swayed together, he pulled her even closer.

"It's good to see you again."

Kelly lifted her head and glanced up at Diamere, then wished she hadn't. His eyes held hers and she couldn't do anything but stare back at him. His good looks mesmerized her. "It's good seeing you, too," she heard herself admit. It was several seconds before either of them spoke again.

"This might sound hard to believe, but this is the first time I've danced at my own club. When I heard that song I knew it was time to do something about that."

"Why is that?"

"I needed an excuse to hold you in my arms again."

Kelly felt a warm rush flow through her midsection

as his piercing gaze continued to bear down on her. "You're making me blush."

"Good," he said as he leaned forward and pressed his lips against her forehead. She shivered. "As long as you're blushing, I know I'm saying the right things."

Kelly lowered her cheek to his chest again. Closing her eyes, she relaxed and allowed the beat of the music to take over. She leaned into Diamere's embrace and let him take the lead, realizing she was more than willing to follow. It felt heavenly to dance in his arms and be so close. She might as well enjoy remembering what it felt like to be held by Diamere Redmond because soon she would be in the backseat of Mark's car, heading home to Wilmington.

The next song was just as slow. Moving closer, she curved her arms around Diamere's neck and enjoyed the rhythm of his hips against hers. Other than swaying from side to side, she had never been much of a slow dancer, but moving with Diamere was easy. As she became caught up in the dance, she found herself wondering what would've happened if things between them had been different. With an exaggerated sniffle, she pushed that ridiculous thought aside. There was no point in wasting energy musing about what-ifs. She had done that way too much in her last relationship and had come to the realization that some things just weren't meant to be. Nevertheless, it didn't stop her from appreciating being held in the arms of the most handsome man in the club. Diamere Redmond was a gorgeous, fun-loving guy, and any woman would be lucky to have him.

The next song was a fast number, and Diamere was skillful and sexy as he moved, spinning Kellis around and pulling her back into his arms. Fast and slow, they went from one dance to another.

"I see you can still dance," Kelly remarked.

"Thanks, you're not half-bad yourself," Diamere said as he escorted her across the balcony. Instead of returning to their table, he led her toward the spiral staircase.

Kelly gave him a curious look. "Where are we going?"

"I want to show you around the club."

Still holding her hand, he led her down the stairs and through the crowd. Kelly noticed several women looking her way, jealousy apparent in their eyes. A warm feeling of pride filled her chest, and it took everything she had not to smile. It felt good being by his side, holding hands as he led her down a long hall. Several people called out Diamere's name. He merely waved or nodded his head. Before long, they were all alone, walking side by side.

"I see you're still quite the popular one. I bet you love getting all that attention," Kelly teased as they stopped outside an elevator.

Turning, Diamere smiled at her as he pushed the up button. "The only attention I want tonight is yours," he said in a low, sexy voice that made her heart skip a beat.

"Stop flirting with me," Kellis managed to say around a smile of her own.

His hand came up to her face and tenderly stroked her cheek. "I merely said what was on my mind."

Her pulse drummed as she breathlessly whispered, "Well, at least you're honest."

"I try to be."

They stepped inside the elevator and Diamere punched numbers on a keypad, sending the car up to the second floor. Leaning his hand on the wall beside Kelly, he gazed down at her and said, "You've known me long enough to know I'm going to tell it like it is. It's best that way. No misunderstandings." He was too close, his mouth too tempting, and with as much as she'd had to drink, Kelly knew she wasn't thinking clearly. Maybe drinking all that alcohol wasn't such a good idea. She was getting in way over her head. Becoming involved with Diamere would be a bad move. Luckily, the elevator doors opened, and she quickly stepped off, savoring the distance. Taking her hand again, Diamere led her down a hallway past a number of offices.

He took her through a suite of plush rooms. As he talked about his business, Kelly realized that Ja'net was more than just a club, it was an investment. Diamere had a full-time marketing coordinator who was responsible for promoting the club, a general manager, a dozen staff members and an efficient twenty-something assistant who brought the staff fresh-baked cookies every Friday. He showed Kelly two large rooms that were used for private parties, both equipped with their own bar and dance floor. As he showed her a large conference room where he met with his staff every Monday, she tried to clear her head. The conversation had shifted to something other than him trying to flirt with her, yet she was having a hard time taking her mind off anything but the sexy man walking beside her. Kelly realized she was only half listening. Her thoughts had wandered into treacherous territories. With Diamere so close, she was too aware of his presence. Tall. Rugged. Broad. She couldn't stop from imagining that body lying across her bed. Just thinking about what was hidden beneath his expensive pants and crisp shirt had her palms sweating. *Snap out of it!* she told herself.

Needing some distance, she moved to a floor-to-ceiling window in the conference room. Outside was a breathtaking view of central Philadelphia.

"You're so beautiful, Kelly."

Upon hearing that, she swung around to find Diamere staring down at her with an intensity that caused her to shiver. His compliment had caught her off guard. Swallowing, she tried to regain her composure. "Thank you," she replied as she watched his gaze lower to her mouth.

Hands in his pants pockets, Diamere moved closer, invading her space, shortening the distance between them. "I should be thanking you."

She felt the pit of her stomach go hot. "Why is that?"

"For allowing me to be in your presence."

Kelly stared up at him for a long, uncomfortable second, then exploded with laughter.

Diamere gave her a sheepish grin. "I guess that did sound a little corny."

"A little?" she said, still giggling. "How about a lot?"

He couldn't help but laugh at his own expense before signaling for her to follow. "Come on. Let me finish showing you around."

At the end of the hall was a pair of double doors. He punched in a code, then turned the lock, and they stepped in. Her eyes traveled around the massive office. It definitely belonged to a man. Dark wood. Heavy burgundy drapes. LCD sixty-inch television in the corner. She chuckled. *Men.*

"I don't spend a lot of time in here, but when I do I need an atmosphere where I can relax and think."

Kelly arched an eyebrow. "I'm sure you do a lot of thinking with that flat-screen in the room."

Diamere tossed his head back and laughed, and Kelly couldn't help but join in.

"Seriously, this place is way more than I expected. You really outdid yourself."

He smiled. "Thanks. I guess we've reached the end of my tour." Diamere slid his hands in his pockets again and rocked on the balls of his feet.

She nibbled her lips nervously. "Yes, I guess we have." Neither made any attempt to move toward the door. Their eyes met.

"Are you seeing anyone?" Diamere asked, breaking the silence.

The air in the room suddenly felt charged. "No, and I prefer to keep it that way."

"Kelly, I'm not looking for commitment. I'm trying to run a business and I don't need the emotional attachment that comes with relationships."

She ignored the butterflies that fluttered in her stomach and pretended his intense gaze didn't affect her. *Liar.* "A man after my own heart. It seems like we still have a lot in common. The last thing I'm looking for is a relationship."

"Good. So there's nothing standing in the way of the two of us getting reacquainted," he said, crossing the room to where she was standing.

Before she could respond, Diamere grasped her hands, pulling her closer. She gasped when she saw where his

thoughts were headed. In a panic, Kelly pushed gently
against his chest. "Dia—"

"Hush," he whispered, and tugged her flush against
his body, then leaned down to cover her mouth with
his.

Chapter 3

Her heart thudded as Diamere's mouth touched hers. And when he parted her lips with his tongue, she knew she had been anticipating this very moment from the second she first spotted him walking toward her in the club. Kelly willingly opened her mouth to him, practically melting when he pulled her closer. Heat danced inside her and her senses whirred dizzily. As their tongues mated, she was only aware of Diamere's mouth against hers, his solid body molded with her own. His tongue flirted with hers, tasting and teasing, until a moan sprang from her throat. Frustrated, she twisted her head away.

"Diamere, please, this is a mistake."

"No, it isn't," he countered, before his thumb grazed her nipple, causing her to cry out. "I've waited a long time to do this."

He lowered her tube top, freeing her heavy breasts,

then dipped down and captured a nipple between his lips. Kelly tossed her head back and moaned. His tongue was warm, wet and tantalizing. He suckled while she unconsciously arched her body and leaned into his mouth. Desire raced through her veins and moisture pooled between her thighs. She knew that if he pushed hard enough they would be making love right here on his dark leather couch. Realizing what she was allowing him to do, she tried again to push away. This time she got this attention.

Diamere looked confused. "What's wrong?"

Embarrassed, Kelly pulled her top back in place. "This *is* a mistake."

"Why?" he asked as he pulled her comfortably into his arms again. "I knew the moment we saw each other this was going to happen. You can't tell me you weren't thinking the same thing."

You don't even know the half of it. The sexual tension was as thick as it could get. And that was the problem. She tried to bury her face against his chest, but Diamere cupped her chin with his hand and raised her head. "Kelly, look at me. I've never forgotten about us," he began as his fingers caressed her cheek. "Things should have been different."

"But they weren't," she said without malice, and pushed against his chest. Diamere released her. Quickly, Kelly moved away and slid her purse back over her shoulder. There was a long, awkward moment of silence. "Thank you for the tour. You have a beautiful club."

"You're welcome." He didn't say anything else, just continued to stare at her with his hands in his pockets, his feet braced apart, making her conscious of how handsome he was.

Nervously, Kelly licked her lips. "Well, I better get going. Essence is probably looking for me."

A satisfied smile curved his mouth. "No, she isn't. She knows you're with me."

And at the moment that was one dangerous place to be.

All Kelly could do was stare up at him wordlessly, not sure what else to say. His expression was intense and she could tell by his eyes what he was thinking.

Reaching out, he captured her hand with his. "I want to continue where we left off," he finally admitted.

His comment caught her off guard and her heart skipped a beat. Kelly pursed her lips and took a deep breath before saying, "I don't think so."

When he didn't bother to comment further, she gave an impatient sigh and made a move to pass him. It was then that she noticed he had not removed his hand from hers. She looked down at it, then back up at his face. A throbbing had started at her temple and she was certain it was a combination of too much alcohol and being around Diamere. The sooner she got away from the club the better off she would be.

"I think it would be a good idea if I went back to my table."

"Why is that?"

She pulled in a rather shaky breath. "Because being around you…alone…I…" She was at a loss for words and getting more frustrated by the moment. "I just think I need to return to my seat."

It frustrated her even more as she watched those thick, sexy lips of his curl upward. "Why? You scared of me?"

Desire twisted inside her as she eyed his mouth.

Remembering how it had tasted, she felt a familiar yearning ripple through her body. Nervously, she gave a strangled laugh. "No, not at all. I just came out tonight to have a good time."

"Are you saying you're not having a good time?"

Her eyes fluttered briefly and she shook her head. "No. I'm having a wonderful time." *More than you'll ever know.* "But it's getting late and I'm ready to head home."

"Then let me take you home," he offered.

Her heartbeat pounded in her ears. "Take me home? I live all the way out in Wilmington. Don't you and your staff people have a club to run?"

"It's one of the advantages of being the boss and having competent employees working for you. Besides, Wilmington is only a thirty-minute drive."

She hesitated and briefly lowered her eyelids. There was no way she was letting him drive her home. Kelly swallowed. "No, really. I can ride back with Essence and my brother."

Diamere looked prepared to counter her response, but instead he nodded and said, "Okay."

Grasping her hand once more, he led her into the hall. This time, instead of taking the elevator, they traveled down a back staircase that took them straight into the club. Music vibrated through Kelly's body, and as she moved across the floor, she wondered if anyone could tell what the two of them had been doing. Self-consciously, she combed her fingers through her hair as she walked beside Diamere. Once they moved up the spiral staircase onto the balcony, she found their table empty, and glanced around for Essence and Mark.

Diamere's eyes traveled over her shoulder. "I don't think they're planning to leave anytime soon."

Kelly swung around and followed the direction of his gaze to the couple on the dance floor, locked in each other's arms with eyes for no one else.

"It looks like you might be here all night."

Seeing the tenderness in Mark's eyes as he lowered his mouth to his wife's parted lips, Kelly swung around and sighed with defeat. "I guess you're right." She brought a hand to her temple. She wasn't sure if it was the alcohol, the music or Diamere, but her head was now pounding worse than before.

He took a step forward, planting himself right in front of her. "After this song, let them know I'm driving you home. Have a seat. I'll be right back. I need to let my manager know I'm rolling out."

Kelly watched him leave and couldn't believe she had essentially agreed to let Diamere take her home. If he offered to do so it was probably because he believed her to be drunk. What in the world was she thinking? She had never been a heavy drinker. Tonight, however, she had been willing to make an exception in an attempt to calm her nerves. Instead, she was going to wake up in the morning with a terrible hangover. "Okay," she said to no one in particular, and took a deep breath. Everything was going to be all right. There was no way Mark and Essence would agree to her leaving with Diamere.

Oh, how wrong she was.

"Oh, sweetie, I hope you feel better in the morning." Essence gave her a big hug.

"Yeah. You're in good hands. I'll check on you tomorrow," Mark added as he bent and kissed her forehead. Then, before Kelly could even voice a protest, he reached for his wife's hand and dragged her back out onto the dance floor.

So much for my big brother looking out for me. With a heavy sigh, she scowled and shook her head. Mark was a fabulous brother. If he thought she was in bad company he would have never allowed her to leave with Diamere. Friend or not.

Kelly slid her purse strap up farther on her shoulder and moved toward the door, where she spotted Diamere shaking hands with a tall man in a dark brown suit. He must be the club manager, she thought. But she didn't have much time to contemplate anything else when Diamere looked up and their eyes locked. *What in the world have I gotten myself into?*

He walked toward her and she felt her body come alive and tingle, starting from her chest and traveling down to more private regions before arriving at her toes. By the time he reached her, her lips were dry and it took everything she had to force herself to swallow.

"You ready?"

Nervously, she dropped her gaze, then realized she was staring at his mouth. *Goodness! What's wrong with me?* She truly wasn't sure, so simply nodded.

Diamere reached down for her hand and escorted her out the door. As soon as they stepped out, a valet handed him the keys to a black Lincoln Navigator SUV. He helped her in, then moved around to the driver's side and pulled away.

They drove for blocks in silence as Kelly stared out the passenger-side window, grateful for the soft R & B music coming through the speakers, because she didn't have a clue what to say to someone she was so desperately trying to fight her attraction for. And after all those drinks, she didn't trust herself to speak. But she watched him out of the corner of her eye. Tall. Handsome. Male. He was staring straight ahead, bobbing his head to the soft beat of the music. She couldn't help wondering what was running through his mind right at that moment. Even though she was sitting on the passenger side, Diamere seemed to be too close, invading her personal space in a way that kept her pulse racing and her mouth dry.

"What's on your mind?"

His voice startled Kelly out of her thoughts. "Why does something have to be on my mind?"

"Because you're so quiet."

She turned to him and smiled. "You are, too, you know."

Diamere hesitated, then briefly looked over at her and laughed. "I guess you're right." He gave another chuckle. "So talk to me. How does it feel being back in Delaware?"

"Good. Really good. What about you?"

"I don't want to be anywhere else," he replied.

She instructed him to take the next exit. Diamere pulled off Highway 95 and came to a stop at a red light.

"Why did you offer to take me home tonight?" she asked.

Diamere turned his head and caught her gaze. Even before he spoke, she could see the answer in his eyes and in the grin on his face. He wanted her! So that's what this drive back to her condo after midnight was all about—a booty call. She fumed. If that was the case, Diamere was in for a rude awakening.

"I wanted to spend a little more time together. Is that

a crime?" He placed his hand over hers and she almost jumped out of her skin at his warm touch.

She shook her head. "Not at all. I truly enjoyed seeing you tonight." Not trusting herself, she turned and looked out the window again. For the rest of the ride, the only time they spoke was when she gave him directions. It didn't take a scientist to know he was thinking the same thing about her as she was about him.

When he pulled in front of her building, she reached for her purse and swung it on her arm. "Thank you so much for the ride."

"No problem."

Diamere climbed out of the car and came around to her side to open her door. Kelly placed her hand in his and allowed him to escort her up the stairs and to her door. After one evening, holding his hand had already begun to feel so natural. But no matter how good it felt, there was no way she was letting him in.

As soon as she turned the key in the lock, she swung around and faced him. Placing her hands on his shoulders, she leaned in and pressed her mouth to his in what was supposed to be a simple peck. However, the second her lips touched his, something exploded between them, causing her to pull back as if she had been burned. "Uh...thanks again," she said, anxious to put the door between them. Otherwise she was liable to do something crazy and invite him inside.

"The pleasure is all mine," Diamere said. Kelly waited for him to release her arm, but instead his grip tightened and he leaned in and whispered, "Before I let you go, I need to give you something."

Kelly knew he was going to kiss her. Her heart started thumping faster.

The first thought that came to Kelly's mind was that she had to resist him. But a second thought quickly followed. Why not go ahead and get him out of her system once and for all? She had to do something. The attraction she felt for him was stronger than any she'd ever felt for a man, and that included Devin Black, the man she had once planned to marry.

As soon as he dipped his head, the thought that whipped through Kelly's mind was that Diamere Redmond was a damn fine kisser. In fact, his kisses had the same impact as those cosmopolitans she'd been drinking all night. Seductive. Intoxicating. She opened her mouth to him and the touch of his tongue to hers sent a jolt through her so intense her midsection suddenly felt like a flaming torch. Overwhelming emotions shot through her and she felt a strange urge to open up to him completely—something she had never felt with a man before, not even her ex-fiancé. Diamere kissed her as if it was his primary purpose in life. He deepened the kiss with skillful strokes of his tongue, staking a possessive claim on her mouth. A claim she didn't want him to make, but one he was making anyway.

Lowering his hands, Diamere cupped her bottom and pressed her so close she had complete contact with his straining arousal. When she wrapped her arms around his neck, he pulled her up, lifting her off the floor and against his body. He tasted like peppermint. It went right to her head and a dizzy feeling of need sent blood rushing through her. When he finally released her mouth and placed her back down on solid ground, they were both breathless. But he didn't let go of her. He continued to hold her tightly in his arms, nibbling at her neck and chin before recapturing her mouth with his for another feverous kiss.

Diamere licked and toyed with her tongue. He sucked and teased passionately, as though he had all the time in the world. He was driving her mad, because the pleasure he aroused was like nothing she had ever experienced before. Potent desire and stimulating sensation radiated from his hands, his tongue and his hard body pressed against hers. When he finally broke off the kiss, she slumped weakly against his chest, thinking that in all her thirty years, she had never been kissed like that.

Kelly slowly regained her senses. She slid her hands from his shoulders and took a step back before tilting her head and meeting his luminous eyes. Without saying a word, Diamere turned and walked away. When he stepped onto the curb, she sighed deeply, still feeling the heat from his kiss.

Diamere walked around to the driver's side of his car, turned to face her, then leaned against the car and waited.

Kelly gazed over at him and nervously moistened her lips. She felt it was safe to assume, after a kiss like that, that Diamere was now out of her system. But it would be a long time before she could ever forget Diamere Redmond.

"Kelly, unless you don't want me to leave, I'd advise you to go inside."

Under the streetlight, she didn't miss the lust burning in his eyes, not to mention the seductive warning in his voice. Obediently, she turned the knob and stepped inside her condo. It wasn't until she shut the door and switched off the porch light that she heard Diamere pull away from the curb.

Kelly crossed the plush, mocha-colored carpet to her bedroom with visions of the evening flashing before her eyes. She had allowed Diamere to hold her in his arms and to kiss her not once but twice. With a moan, she pressed a hand to her temple. What in the world was she thinking? That was the problem. She wasn't thinking. She was going to regret everything, especially the alcohol, in the morning.

Lowering herself onto her peach satin comforter, she kicked off her shoes and lay back on the bed, staring up at the ceiling fan above. She could still feel the firmness of his mouth against hers. Unconsciously she pressed her fingertips to her tingling lips and exhaled. Diamere was back in Philadelphia and he was now single. The knowledge of both these things made her heart pound so hard she had to gasp for air. A relationship was the last thing she needed. There were too many other things that were way too important. Besides, the last time she'd decided to put her heart on the line for a man, she got burned.

Diamere and Devin are two different men.

That was true. Diamere had qualities to which Devin couldn't even begin to compare. Kelly knew Diamere, and if she had to, she could trust him with her life. But her heart? No way. She wouldn't be a fool again.

Realizing she was being ridiculous, she rose from the bed and moved into the adjoining bathroom for a quick shower. Diamere had made it clear he wasn't looking for anything serious, and neither was she. A year ago she had learned a hard lesson—love, the happily-ever-after kind, existed only in romance novels.

Chapter 4

I have twenty-two children.

Looking down at the roster, Kelly couldn't help the smile on her face. In four weeks she would be starting her teaching career at Baer Elementary School for the second time. Staring at the names, she shook her head. Six months ago she never would have guessed she would be back in Delaware.

She rose from her chair and moved down the aisle between small metal desks and chairs as she tried to push the painful memories aside. If things had gone along as planned, a week from Friday would have been her wedding day. Kelly released a heavy sigh of despair. Two years ago, she'd decided she needed a change, and had relocated to San Antonio, Texas, hoping to begin a new life. It wasn't long before she had started dating Devin Black, a fifth-grade science teacher. She thought he was everything she had wanted, and was willing to give him just about everything she had to offer, except for one thing she held dear to her heart. Her virginity.

With the values her mother had instilled in her, Kelly believed that love and sex came hand in hand, and refused to take any relationship to the next level until she was certain she loved the man she was with and they had a future together. After six months of dating, to her delight, Devin had confessed his love and dropped down on one knee in the teacher's lounge in front of half the staff and proposed. Tears flooded her eyes as Kelly nodded her head and happily accepted. It was barely two weeks later when she decided that maybe it was time to move their relationship to the next level. She loved Devin enough to give him the greatest gift of all.

She had stayed late grading papers, and knew Devin was still somewhere in the building. Eager to share her news, Kelly had gone in search of him to invite him away for a weekend of passion. Not finding him in his classroom, she'd walked down to the teacher's lounge and found him in a compromising position with the art instructor.

Devastated, Kelly had finished out the end of the school year, then handed in her resignation and returned home. She vowed that never again would she give her heart to a man for him to stomp on. Devin had been the second man she had ever loved and the second to break her heart. She had been a fool one time too many.

Diamere didn't mean to break your heart.

Shaking her head, Kelly tried to free her mind of memories of the weekend. But no matter how much she tried, Diamere always found a way to invade her thoughts. She wasn't interested in another relationship. However, ever since she'd looked up to see him staring at her with those intense chocolate-brown eyes, she'd been reminded that she was a woman. It had been four days since Diamere had kissed her, yet her lips tingled each and every time she was foolish enough to remember.

"It's lunchtime."

Kelly glanced over at the door as Essence walked into her classroom. She would be teaching a class of fourth-graders, two doors down.

"I guess you're right," Kelly replied as she looked up at the clock on the wall. "What do you have a taste for today?"

"How about we go to Clarence's?"

She nodded eagerly at the suggestion. "That definitely sounds like a winner." Clarence's Infamous Chicken and Fish House was a reputable soul food chain known all across the state of Delaware. Rising from her chair, she reached for a small briefcase and started stuffing in papers from her desk. She still had quite a bit to do before the school season began, and had no problem taking work home.

"Have you heard from Diamere?" Essence asked as she waited for her.

Kelly paused long enough to meet Essence's curious eyes before dropping her gaze again. "No, but I don't expect to. I told you we're just friends."

Her sister-in-law frowned, arms folded across her chest. "Kelly, who are you trying to fool? I hope not me. I was there. I know how crazy you were about Diamere and how devastated you were when he decided to marry Ryan." Her gaze narrowed. "I thought you wanted him more than anything in the world? Yeah, yeah, I know. Well, guess what? He's single now and this is your chance."

Kelly groaned at the reminder. She had once confided in Essence that she had been in love with him since eighth grade, and would do anything for him to notice her as a woman. A lump formed in her throat as she recalled that painful night seven years ago. Diamere had come to her and told her his ex-girlfriend was pregnant, and that he was going to marry her because he didn't want his child to grow up without a father. Back then Kelly had felt as if the world had come crashing down on her. Even now she could feel the pain as if it had been just yesterday.

She cleared her throat. "That was before Ryan got pregnant and had the twins." Hearing Essence snort rudely and mumble something under her breath, she looked up. "What?"

Essence pursed her lips. "Those weren't his kids."

"What?" she gasped, head spinning with confusion. "Okay, first you tell me Diamere is no longer married. Now you're saying the twins weren't his?" When Essence nodded, Kelly paused long enough to shake her head. "Okay, you need to back up and start from the beginning." Kelly came around and leaned on the edge of her desk. While her friend explained the chain of events, she stood there with her mouth opened, stunned by everything she heard. "Oh, no! How can someone do something like that?" she cried, shaking her head.

"She is someone who only cares about herself."

Kelly shook her head again, trying to digest what she had just heard. "I can only imagine how he is feeling."

Shifting her weight, Essence added, "He was devastated about losing the girls. They meant everything to him. Every time he called the house he had something new to tell us. As a matter of fact..." she allowed her voice to trail off as she reached inside her purse and removed her wallet "…here's a picture he sent us in a Christmas card last year."

Kelly took the small photo and a smile curled her lips as she stared down at the precious little identical faces. The back read "Tanisha and Nichole, age five." With such large brown eyes, naturally long lashes and deep dimples, they were going to be heartbreakers. *Just like their mother,* Kelly thought. Because that was exactly what Ryan had done—broken Diamere's heart. As she handed the photo back, Kelly pressed her lips together bitterly. She got angry just thinking about what that woman had done to him.

"Now that that mess is over, I would love to see the two of you finally get together."

Kelly gave a dismissive wave. "That's the past. We're different people now."

"Not that different," Essence insisted. "He's a good man."

Kelly had no doubt that he was. But if she were to get involved with Diamere, there would be hard feelings, or even worse, regret. And there was her own issue of not being able to separate her body from her heart, which was why she had managed to stay a virgin all these years.

"He's a family man."

Kelly shook her head in objection. "He's not looking for anything serious."

Essence tapped her foot impatiently on the tile floor. "No, but then neither are you. So why not enjoy each other's company?"

With a heavy sigh, Kelly pulled herself up, then moved back behind her desk and finished gathering her papers. Maybe Essence was right. Maybe it wasn't too late for them. Maybe the two of them could enjoy each other. This way she could finally close that chapter in her life. But the mere thought of allowing herself to fall under another man's spell frightened her. She'd made that mistake with Devin and knew where that had gotten her. On the other hand, the thought of giving in to her feelings and sharing her bed with Diamere was tempting, to say the least. Her stomach quivered at the thought of finally making love. Quickly, Kelly dismissed that idea. It was too much. She was probably the oldest living virgin around. Unfortunately, there was no way she could separate her body from her heart. Not when Diamere was involved. Her feelings for him ran too deep. Nevertheless, the thought of never knowing what it could be like between them was enough to drive her insane.

"Maybe," she heard herself say.

"Maybe?" Essence tossed her hands in the air. "I don't know what I'm going to do with you!"

Kelly chuckled. "He didn't even ask me for my phone number."

"Do you really think it's that hard? All Diamere has to do is pick up the phone and call my house."

"And is that supposed to make me feel better?" she said with a strangled laugh. "Diamere could reach me if he wanted. And apparently he doesn't. It's been four days since he brought me home and he hasn't tried to call me once." Unconsciously, each and every time the phone rang, Kelly had half expected it to be him, and was disappointed when it wasn't. "If he's interested he would've called by now."

"And what if he doesn't?"

Their eyes connected before Kelly shrugged. "Then it wasn't meant to be."

"So you're just going to sit back and let some hoochie get her claws in him?" At Kelly's silence, Essence continued. "I don't know if you know this or not, but a woman can ask a man out. Come on," she coaxed.

Immediately, Kelly shook her head. "Not me. I'm old-fashioned." There was no way she was setting herself up for failure. "If he's interested in seeing me again, he will call." Tired of talking about him, she added, "Enough of this, anyway. I'm hungry. Let me grab my purse." She pulled open her desk drawer and removed a small white designer bag she had been delighted to find on sale last month.

Kelly swung the strap over her shoulder and reached for her briefcase. "I can't believe I'm saying this, but I'll be glad when the summer is over and the school year starts. Four more weeks."

Essence met her smile and gave a knowing look. "Neither can I." It was going to be her first year back at Baer Elementary School, as well. When the principal had found out that both of them wanted to return, he didn't hesitate in giving them positions. As far as Principal Combs was concerned, both women had reputations for being fabulous educators who cared about their students. And their school strived for excellence.

Together they exited the rear of the building, the quickest route out to the parking lot. As she neared her car, Kelly stopped in her tracks when she spied a man leaning against the bumper of her Saturn. Diamere! Her pulse raced at the sight of him. When he spotted them, he straightened and started heading their way, while Kelly felt all kinds of flutters in her stomach.

He waved and Essence returned the gesture. "Hey, Diamere!" she cried, with a little too much emphasis, making Kelly wonder if maybe this was another set-up.

"Hello, ladies." He offered them a warm smile.

Kelly cleared the lump from her throat. "Diamere, what are you doing here?"

He slowed his stride and gave her that warm dimpled grin she had loved for years. "I thought I'd drop by and see if I could possibly take my favorite schoolteacher to lunch."

Stunned beyond words, Kelly looked to Essence for help. When she finally realized she wasn't getting any, she found the words to say, "Essence and I were just about to go and eat."

As if on cue, her sister-in-law reached for her cell phone. "Actually, Mark just texted me and said he's home early. So I'll go and have lunch with him. But you two have fun. I'll call you later." She waved as she strolled to her car before Kelly had a chance to get a word in.

Great. Just great.

"You look good," Diamere told her appreciatively.

"Thanks." Kelly had no choice but to look at him, and when she did she swayed slightly. Diamere was wearing a pair of jeans shorts that hugged his toned thighs, and an orange polo-style shirt that emphasized his broad chest. She loved a man in orange. On his feet were expensive brown leather sandals.

"So? How about sharing lunch with me?"

Kelly stared into his mesmerizing eyes while contemplating her answer. *You know you want to go!* Of course, that didn't necessarily mean it was the right decision. So why in the world wasn't her body listening? she thought as she felt her traitorous head nodding.

"Good," he replied, looking more than pleased by her answer. Kelly made no attempt to move, and after a long, awkward moment, Diamere cleared his throat and reached for her briefcase. "I don't know about you, but it's hot out here. Come on. Your chariot awaits."

Diamere loaded Kelly's briefcase in the trunk of her Saturn, then escorted her over to his SUV. He opened the door and watched while she slipped onto the leather seat and reached for the seat belt. His admiring gaze lingered provocatively. A man who appreciated a good-looking woman, he had no choice but to glance down to her long, shapely legs. They were as toned as the legs of any professional female athlete. Kelly had always been a physically active woman, but he couldn't help but notice how shapely her thighs and calves were. When she had first stepped out through the double doors of the school, Diamere had sucked in his breath at the sight of her in a peach seersucker dress that stopped well above her knees. With legs like that she could put any girl ten years younger to shame.

Seeing Kelly again was doing a number on him. He couldn't recall ever wanting a woman so badly. Short. Petite. She was supersexy, but that was only a fraction of her appeal. He was drawn to her energy and her enthusiasm. Kelly had once been the biggest spark in his otherwise gloomy life. And after seeing her on Friday, he'd realized that quality was just as strong as ever. The last few days he had found himself thinking more and more about her, and it always managed to bring a smile to his lips.

Diamere took a long, deep breath, forcing himself to breathe normally and get his emotions under control. He realized what was happening between them and wondered if Kelly realized it, as well. He had a feeling she did when she noticed him staring at her and broke eye contact quickly, looking down at her lap. Luckily for him, she wasn't quick enough. He saw the contemplative look in her eyes.

Confidently, Diamere took another deep breath. Life had taught him that if you wanted something, then you needed to do everything in your power to get it. If you waited around for it to come to you, you'd never have it. He was a man who believed in getting what he wanted, which was why he had come to take Kelly to lunch.

"Are you ready to get going?"

He glanced at her smiling face. Damn, he wasn't sure how long he had been staring, making a fool of himself. "Yeah, um…sure."

Diamere shifted and made himself comfortable behind the wheel. "I hope you like Clarence's?"

Kelly turned her head toward him, eyes sparkling with amusement. "I love it. In fact, that's where Essence and I were going to go before you arrived."

Diamere put on his seat belt, but hesitated before starting the car. "I didn't mean to interrupt your lunch plans. If you'd rather eat with Essence than me, I understand."

"No, I'd be happy to have lunch with you."

"Good," he replied, happy with her answer. He turned the key in the ignition and a rush of cool air circulated through the vents. The temperature was already well over eighty degrees and it was barely noon. He maneuvered the luxury SUV through the residential neighborhood in the direction of the small, popular restaurant.

"So are you playing hooky today? Wait, I forgot. You're the boss."

He took a quick glance at Kelly and chuckled. "I see you've still got your sense of humor. Actually, I had some business to take care of in Wilmington. I finished early so I thought I would swing by to see if I could steal you away for lunch."

"I'm glad you did."

Pleased by her confession, he smiled.

On the ride to the restaurant, just a few blocks away, they chatted about the weather and the upcoming school year before Kelly steered the conversation back to them.

"How did you know what time I left for lunch?"

Diamere took his eyes off the road long enough to admit, "I called Mark last night. Essence grabbed the phone and told me."

Kelly flipped her hair away from her face and blushed prettily. "I'm gonna kill that girl," she replied, then added, "but, really, I'm glad you came by."

Diamere pulled into the parking lot and brought the car to a stop. Her honesty caused unexpected warmth to surge through him. He knew Kelly was attracted to him. He could see it in her eyes. It was also obvious in the kisses they had shared a few nights ago. Yet it still felt as if she put up a brick wall with a sign that said Predators Beware. Her comment gave him hope that maybe he was getting somewhere.

He turned in his seat. "To be totally honest, I was looking for an excuse to see you." From the look on her face, Diamere could tell his response surprised her.

"Why?"

He met her eyes. "Because I haven't been able to stop thinking about you since Friday." He couldn't stop looking at her, either—at those earthy cinnamon eyes. Did she realize her mere presence kept him hot and aroused? No longer able to resist, Diamere leaned over and pressed his lips against hers. Light and affectionate, his mouth just touched hers, yet he experienced an explosive sensation. Smiling, he drew back. Diamere could sense her breath quickening. Good. He wasn't the only one who felt desire brewing wildly between them. Confident he had given her enough to think about, he opened his door and climbed out.

Chapter 5

Kelly barely had time to take two deep breaths before Diamere opened her door. Butterflies fluttered in her stomach and dizziness still lingered from their kiss. He took her hand and she stepped out of the SUV, pulse racing. *Get it together,* she kept telling herself. She had no plans to fall for this man again, and knew she needed to keep her head straight to accomplish that. The last thing she needed was for Diamere to think she was the least bit interested in a relationship.

He shut the door, but instead of releasing her, he laced his fingers with hers and led her to the restaurant. As soon as they stepped inside, the smell of catfish hit her nose and her stomach growled.

"I'm glad to know I'm not the only one who's hungry," Diamere teased.

She giggled and followed him to a table near the window.

The place was already busy with the lunch rush. Kelly took a seat in the chair Diamere offered to her, and rested her hands on the red-and-white-checkered tablecloth. Glancing around the room, she eyed the rhythm and blues photos and memorabilia mounted on the walls until their waitress arrived with their menus. A pretty twenty-something, her face lit up the instant she spotted Diamere.

"Hey, Diamere!" she exclaimed merrily.

He smiled with recognition. "How are you doing, Tammy? How're the boys?"

She rolled her eyes. "They're a handful, but we're all doing great."

Diamere looked over at Kelly. "Tammy, this is my good friend Kelly. Tammy is one of my former employees," he explained.

Kelly shook her proffered hand. "It's a pleasure to meet you."

"Same here," she said, then changed to her professional mode. "Today's special is catfish, shrimp and coleslaw, for five ninety-nine."

Kelly looked at Diamere and nodded. "That sounds good to me."

He held up his fingers. "Make that two. And I'll also take a sweetened tea."

"Me, too," Kelly stated.

Tammy scribbled across a small pad. "All right. Two specials with iced teas, coming right up."

As soon as she moved toward the kitchen, Diamere leaned forward and said in a low voice, "She's really come a long way."

Kelly looked at him with interest. "What do you mean?"

"She was in an abusive relationship with her husband for years. After seeing one black eye too many, I told her either she had to leave the bastard or I was going to personally kill him and make her a widow," he replied with sympathy and anger pooling in his eyes. "Thank God she took her boys and left him. He tried to get her back but she finally stood strong and divorced him."

"Thank goodness for that."

Diamere nodded and leaned back in the chair. "She was one of my best employees."

Curious, Kelly crossed her arms. "Then why doesn't she still work for you?"

The corner of his lips tilted upward. "I used to own this restaurant."

"What? You owned…" Her voice trailed off as she suddenly remembered something. "This used to be your father's restaurant." She recalled that Darren Redmond used to own a successful family restaurant, one she had eaten in on at least two occasions.

Diamere nodded. "Yep. But after my dad passed away I decided the restaurant business was not for me, so I sold it to my cousin, Bianca Beaumont, and her husband, London Brown, who happens to own the Clarence's Infamous Chicken and Fish House franchise."

"Wow!" Kelly cried, then glanced around the room. "I've been here many times before but it never even dawned on me that this was the same restaurant."

His eyes also traveled around and his smile widened. "It's the same place, just a different look. I still have part ownership, but I now focus all my attention on the three women in my life."

Kelly gave him a puzzled look. "Three women?"

"Ja'net, Diamond and Hadley. I have to put business first, you know."

She laughed as Diamere tried to keep a straight face, but eventually he gave in and laughed along with her. Tammy returned with their drinks and Kelly thanked her, then brought the straw to her lips and sipped. "Wow! This tea is really good."

"That's why folks buy it by the gallon."

They talked about the restaurant until their food arrived. Kelly's stomach growled again the second Tammy lowered the plate to the table. As soon as she was gone, Kelly bit into the fried fish and couldn't resist a moan. No one battered seafood like Clarence's. "What made you decide to buy a nightclub—or, correction, three?" she asked, breaking the momentary silence.

"Opportunity," Diamere told her between bites. "A friend of mine was trying to sell the clubs to cover his brother's legal fees. I jumped at the chance. Renovated the places and changed the dress codes, and a year later I've got three of the hottest clubs in Philadelphia."

She smiled, happy for his success. "I'm proud of you."

"Thanks. I put a lot of hours into my business. After Ryan and I divorced, I needed something to take my mind off of her and the twins."

"Essence told me what happened. I'm so sorry," Kelly said apologetically.

"Thanks. I really miss those girls and tried to be a part of their lives, but their real father flat-out refused." Diamere stabbed a shrimp with his fork. "Them's the breaks. You know what they say—once, shame on her, twice, shame on me. All I know is I'll never set myself up for failure again."

She didn't miss the hint of bitterness in his voice. Kelly knew exactly what he meant. She had been foolish once, as well, giving her heart to a man, and had even been ready to give him the most precious gift a woman ever could give a man—her virginity. Thank goodness she had found out the truth in time.

"What's your story? Last I heard you were living in Texas and getting married."

She met his gaze. "It was before I realized I was about to make a terrible mistake. I walked in on my fiancé and another woman."

"Ouch."

"Right." Kelly finished chewing, then shrugged. "After that I realized I truly missed being home."

"Any regrets?"

She met his intense look and felt her insides turn liquid. "Nope. No regrets. I finally found the right path. I'm back here teaching and going to Wilmington University at night, working on my master's degree."

"Good for you."

"Thanks. Our assistant principal is leaving at the end of the first semester. Her husband got a job in Los Angeles and she's going with him. I'm planning to apply for her job."

"That's great, but I thought you liked teaching."

She had asked herself that same question several times while she had been weighing the pros and cons. "As long as I'm still working with the students, I'll be happy. And this way I can work with a whole lot of them."

While they finished their lunch they talked about her upcoming school semester and how she planned to take a few days to go down to Rehoboth Beach to her grandparents' summer home. That would be the only vacation she'd have all year, although she planned to spend the majority of the time working on her thesis.

After Diamere took care of the bill, he escorted her out to the SUV and they drove back to the school in silence. Kelly had to admit she'd had a fabulous time with him. Even after all these years, Diamere was still the same carefree man with an amazing personality.

He pulled in beside her Saturn, then came around and opened the door for her. Kelly stepped out of the Navigator and tried to get past him, but Diamere was blocking her way. Suddenly, she became nervous. "Thanks for lunch."

"The pleasure was all mine."

The word *pleasure* had a weird effect on her and she felt her insides quiver. Pleasure was something she was desperately missing in her life.

They gazed at each other for a long, intense moment before he said, "I'd like to take you to dinner and a movie on Friday."

His offer shocked her. She met his eyes and tried not to drown in their depth. "Why?" Her heart was now beating frantically. If she didn't get away from him she was going to do something foolish, like allow him to kiss her again.

Diamere took a step closer. "Why?" He smiled. "Do you really have to ask why? Because we have some unfinished business."

The air around them snapped, crackled and popped with sexual tension. The look he gave her told her he was thinking about the last night they had spent together seven years ago, and how close she had come to giving in to her desires and allowing him to...

Kelly shook off the thought. There was no way they could go back to that day. What happened was in the past and needed to stay there. So much had happened since then. They had both changed and were two different people. She tried swallowing and ran her sweaty hands across her hips. "I think some things are better left alone," she said, barely above a whisper.

"I disagree." He lifted a hand to her waist and brought her body flush against his. "If things hadn't happened the way they had... If Ryan hadn't..." He drew a deep breath and Kelly knew he was trying to keep his cool as he tried not to remember what that woman had put him through. "I just want to finish where we left off."

She licked her lips nervously. "We're not the same people."

"Maybe not, but we're both still attracted to each other and that's not about to go away." He pulled her tighter. "How about at least agreeing to have dinner with me?"

Kelly had to tilt her head to meet his eyes, and gave Diamere a light nod.

"I knew you would."

Before she could say anything, Diamere dropped his lips down on hers, his tongue effortlessly opening her to him, and then she felt it. Passion. And when his tongue touched hers, she heard a moan. It took her a second before she realized it had come from her. She brought her arms around his neck, locked her fingers together and leaned in closer. The blood surged through her veins, lowering her resistance and blotting out all the reasons why kissing him again was wrong. Right now none of that mattered. She let him kiss her, let him taste her. His lips were hot and urgent and so damn irresistible. This was what she had been longing for the past several days. His taste. His smell. The feel of his body next to hers. He pulled her closer and yet it still wasn't close enough as far as she was concerned. Everything else around them vanished and at that exact moment nothing else existed except for Diamere kissing her.

As the kiss deepened, all Kelly could think about were her wants and desires, and right now she wanted desperately to feel his mouth on hers, his tongue dancing with hers, his body pressing against hers. Diamere slid his hands down her back, rounding her hips and cupping the swell of her bottom as he lifted her gently off her feet. Another helpless moan slid from her lips. The man had skills. He deepened the kiss and she felt shock and excitement all tangled up in one—a magnificent sensation.

Pulling her even closer, Diamere pressed Kelly against his arousal. Knowing how badly he wanted her drove her even crazier. She wanted him, too. His hand slid around the front of her dress and cupped the swell of her aching breasts. Through the seersucker fabric, Kelly could feel the heat of his touch. His hand was kneading, stroking while his index finger circled the sensitive peaks straining in response against her cotton bra. Kelly wanted him. She wanted him so badly her body was humming with a need she had never felt before…and that was a problem.

Her eyes flew open and she pushed hard against his chest. "Diamere, please!" she cried finally. "We're acting like kids!"

"Well, we are in an elementary school parking lot." He laughed as if sincerely amused.

"Ha ha! Very funny," Kelly replied as she pulled her dress back into place. What in the world was she thinking, allowing him to ravish her in the parking lot of her school? What if Principal Combs witnessed the two of them acting like a pair of horny teenagers? Angry more at herself than at him, she wiped her mouth and met his eyes with a stern look. "Look, thanks for lunch, but I need to go before I end up losing my job."

Diamere caught her arm just as she brushed past him. "Kelly, wait. I'm sorry. I'll agree that things did get a little out of hand here, but there's something about you that makes it hard for me to behave properly when you're around."

She saw the sincerity in his eyes, and knew what he meant firsthand. She had no control over her own emotions when she was around him, either.

"No harm done," she replied, then looked over at the school to make sure Principal Combs's office window wasn't in plain view, sighing with relief when it wasn't.

"Hey, why don't you let me make it up to you and take you to a movie on Friday?"

Her brows rose. "What happened to dinner?"

His laugh was deep, warm and rich. "That, too. You can even have some popcorn if you want it."

Smiling, she turned on her heel and moved toward her car. "I might just take you up on that offer. I'll be in touch."

Chuckling, he called after her, "Don't keep me waiting too long."

Kelly climbed into her car feeling better than she had in months. She would let Diamere sweat a little even though she had every intention of spending Friday evening with him. At the blink of an eye, Diamere Redmond had managed to wiggle his way back into her life. She wasn't prepared yet to admit how she felt about that. But one thing was for sure—no matter what happened between them, she would never allow him to get close to her heart.

Chapter 6

On Wednesday, Diamere strolled into Hadley, located in downtown Philadelphia, shortly after ten o'clock in the morning. His secretary, Peaches, was already behind the desk with the phone to her ear. As soon as she saw him, she mouthed, "Good morning," and held up a stack of telephone messages. He gave her a warm smile and took the pink slips of paper from her hand, thumbing through them as he moved into his large corner office and sat behind his mahogany desk. The callers were mostly alcohol sales representatives, eager to retain his business. As he reached the end of the stack, he paused at the only personal message. Ernestine Redmond, aka Nana. He had to smile. His grandmother had made sure Peaches wrote down a reminder that he was not to miss the annual recreational dance at the retirement home.

Two years ago, he'd had a fit when Nana mentioned selling his childhood home and moving into a fifty-five-plus retirement community. But after his grandfather's death, Diamere realized that just because Pops had died, Nana hadn't. In the last year he'd seen the eighty-five-year-old woman happier than she'd been since his grandfather had grown ill from liver disease and eventually passed away. Diamere visited Nana often at the retirement home and even attended a couple of social events, and of course was a hit with the ladies. The August dance was in two weeks. Diamere chuckled. There was no way he could forget. Peaches had left reminder messages on his computer, BlackBerry hand-held and office calendar.

Diamere set the messages aside and logged on to his computer. The middle of the week was when he took care of all the business needs of his nightclubs. He had offices in all three, but Hadley was the most central location and where he spent the majority of his time conducting business.

"I was wondering if you were coming in today."

He glanced up at his manager, whose massive chest and arms blocked the doorway, and grinned. Tony had been working for him since he opened for business. And not a day had passed that Diamere hadn't thanked his lucky stars. "You forget I'm the boss." Laughing, he rocked back in the chair. "How'd things go last night?" Tuesday was karaoke night at Hadley.

Shaking his head, Tony straightened in the doorway. "Nice crowd. I think the contest is really drawing people in."

Diamere noted the lines at the corners of his mouth. "Good, then why the frown?" They'd been running a karaoke contest for the last three weeks. The top singer would win a VIP membership for one year, which included reserved parking in a prime spot out front.

Tony snorted as he moved into the office and approached the desk. "Because I had to let Carlos go last night. He was drunk again."

Diamere lifted a brow. Carlos was one of his best bartenders. Unfortunately, he had an alcohol problem and had been caught on more than one occasion drinking on the job. Diamere had brought him into his office twice and counseled him before Carlos finally left him no choice but to give him a clear written warning that the next time he was caught drinking he would be terminated. It looked like that time had finally come.

"Carlos got into a shouting match with a customer who complained that he had mixed his drink incorrectly. Instead of making him another, Carlos argued with the man that he had been making drinks long enough to know how to make a proper dry martini. It was pretty embarrassing."

Diamere gave him a hard stare. "I hope you calmed the customer."

Tony nodded. "Yes. I apologized and gave him free drinks for the rest of the night and two VIP passes for him and a friend for the duration of the month."

"Good job." Customer service was important to Diamere. He didn't take it lightly and expected the same of all his employees.

"I've already faxed an ad to the newspaper for a replacement."

"Excellent. If Carlos gives you any problems just tell him to come and see me."

"I'll do just that." Tony rose. "By the way, we're already out of Grey Goose vodka."

"We've got a lot of vodka drinkers in Philly," Diamere said with a grin as he remembered one beauty in particular who loved cosmopolitans. "The distributor should be in later this afternoon. Go ahead and order an extra case."

"Got it, boss."

Diamere's phone rang just as Tony excused himself and moved down the hall to his own office. "Hadley, Diamere Redmond speaking."

"You know I hate having to call you at work. Why don't you ever answer your home phone when your grandmother calls?"

A smile curled his lips at the sound of Ernestine Redmond's voice. "Because I'm never at home, Nana. I told you, you can always reach me on my cell phone."

She gave a snort. "That's way too many numbers to remember."

"Nana, I programmed it on your speed dial."

"You kids and your technology. I'm lucky I remember to put my teeth in in the morning."

He chuckled softly. "I got the messages you left with Peaches this morning. I just didn't have a chance to call you."

"Nice girl. Although, what was her mother thinking, calling her Peaches? Sounds like a piece of fruit or something."

Diamere laughed out loud. His nana was definitely something else.

He had spent a lot of time with his grandmother, growing up, when his mother decided to go back to work after ten years of being a homemaker. Nana had been everything a grandmother should be—warm, caring and considerate—although Diamere knew firsthand that the feisty little woman wasn't a pushover.

"Have you heard from my mother?" he asked curiously.

"Yes, she called me while visiting some country I couldn't even begin to pronounce, and said she was having the time of her life. I guess I'll have to go with her next year."

Diana Redmond was currently on a seventeen-day cruise of the Mediterranean with her seniors travel club. It was supposed to have been a mother-daughter vacation, but at the last minute Nana had declined. "How are you feeling?" he asked, suddenly concerned about her health.

"Fabulous for an old lady."

Diamere rested his elbow on the desk. "I'm glad to hear it. If you're calling to remind me about the August dance, I haven't forgotten."

"Good, but that's not why I phoned. I'm doing a head count for the buffet and wanted to know if you were bringing a date."

Oh, boy. "I wasn't planning on bringing anyone."

"It would please a dying old woman if you did."

"Nana, you're not dying."

She snorted rudely. "Fiddlesticks. I'm eighty-five years old. God could come calling tomorrow, and I want to at least see you happy before I leave for heaven."

"I am happy."

"Oh, for heaven's sake! I want to see you happy with a good woman by your side, baking you cakes and pies."

"Now, Nana, if I had some woman doing that, what would be left for you to do?"

"Hug and kiss my great-grandbabies."

He knew how hurt she had been when they'd found out the twins weren't really his. Ryan, who'd always had a soft spot for Ernestine, had been at least compassionate enough to agree to still bring the twins up to see her when in Philadelphia visiting her parents.

"Could you at least think about bringing a date?"

Diamere blew out a defeated breath. "Okay, I'll think about it."

"Good. I'll mark you down for two."

He chuckled, then listened as she told him about one of the residents getting caught skinny-dipping in the pool, before Nana finally hung up to watch her soap operas.

As he skimmed through his e-mails, Diamere found himself thinking about his grandmother's request. A date. Bringing a woman to meet Nana was something he didn't believe in doing unless he was serious. He didn't want to give any woman the wrong impression. After Ryan, marriage was definitely the last thing on his mind. He wouldn't say he'd never get married again, but it wasn't a road he was interested in traveling anytime soon.

As he thought about possible dates, he realized there wasn't anyone he'd gone out with in the last six months that he would even consider taking to the dance. Most of the women he met weren't interested in a strictly sexual, no-strings-attached relationship. In his thirty-five years he'd run into every type of female imaginable. After several regrets he'd figured out how to weed out the needy, clingy women and the ones who sought commitment. Then there were the ones in it for the money. But he rarely found a woman who wasn't looking for anything other than a few laughs and some sweet loving on occasion.

Diamere laced his fingers behind his head as he thought about the past several months. After his breakup with Ryan, he'd vowed to never become involved in another serious relationship. And to insure there were no misunderstandings, he was honest with women from day one that he wasn't looking for anything long-term. He made it his policy to never date women who frequented his club or worked for him. Both were recipes for disaster. But he was a natural flirt. He knew that and couldn't do anything about it. It was part of his charm. Nevertheless, he didn't need a woman watching his every move and getting upset if he paid someone else a little too much attention. As far as he was concerned it was good customer service. That's why dating a woman where he worked was definitely a no-no. Inviting one back to his place was out, as well. The last thing he needed was someone popping up unannounced. Nope. None of the women he dated knew where he lived, and he preferred it that way.

Until now.

Diamere leaned back in his seat as a particular slender beauty came to mind. Kelly was different from all of those other women. Part of it was because he had known her for almost half his life, and that in itself made her special. His door would always be open to her.

Staring out the window, he thought about inviting Kelly to his place and how welcome he wanted her to feel. So comfortable that she'd be lying across his bed, naked, waiting.... Diamere groaned at the sudden heat that traveled to his loins. He was torturing himself, but he truly couldn't get her off his mind. Their last kiss still haunted him. He remembered pulling back and staring down at her lips, which were moist, swollen, parted. And then there had been those luminous cinnamon eyes that widened so expressively. She had felt it, too. There was no denying the heat and passion burning between them.

His lips curled at the thought of her beautiful mocha face. Ever since lunch at Clarence's he'd been thinking about her. One thing he had always admired about Kelly was that she had no idea how beautiful she really was. He also loved the way she tried to act as if she wasn't attracted to him. The way she blushed when he asked her out and the way she tried to deny what she was feeling. She made it clear she wasn't looking for anything long-term. And that was perfect. He missed her smile. Holding her in his arms. Her touch. Her taste. Friday couldn't come soon enough.

Dammit, he thought. He was doing it again. Getting ahead of himself. So far Kelly hadn't even called to confirm their date. *Oh, brother.* He now had a serious hard-on and the only woman who could satisfy him was Kelly. Soon kisses wouldn't be enough. He was going to want to explore her body and get to know it well. For years he'd admired her from a distance, and now he wanted to examine her up close. She aroused everything about him that was male, and he knew whatever type of relationship they decided to share, it would be different from anything he'd had with any other woman.

Without thinking, Diamere picked up the phone and dialed Mark's cell. While he waited for him to answer, he chuckled. In all this haste to get to know Kelly again, he'd forgotten to ask for her phone number.

* * *

Kelly stepped into her condo and immediately slipped her mules off her feet, padding barefoot toward her bedroom at the end of the hallway. While she moved, she quickly thumbed through her mail and paused at the last piece—a light blue envelope. Her address had been typed and there was no return address. Her lips twisted. She had a pretty good idea who the card was from. Quickly, she took a seat on her queen-size bed and broke the seal with one French nail. She slipped out the card and read it.

"Please forgive me and the error of my ways. I still love you."

Kelly pursed her lips and tossed the card aside. There was no point in reading any more. It was from Devin, and she didn't want to hear or read anything he had to say. This wasn't the first time he'd tried to contact her. No, there had been so many phone calls that she had been forced to change her number. There had been so many flowers and gifts, all of which found their way to the nearest trash can. *The same place this card is going,* she thought as she moved back down the hall to her large, spacious kitchen and removed a bottle of water from the stainless steel refrigerator. Just thinking about Devin made her blood boil. Did he really think she would forgive him after what he had done to her? She snorted at the thought and took a swallow of water. Her mama hadn't raised a fool. There was no way in the world Kelly would ever consider taking him back. That was one pain she wished to never feel again, which was why she had no intention of letting another man get that close to her.

The phone on the wall rang, startling her to the point

that she choked on a swig of water. She reached for the receiver and coughed until she found the breath to say, "Hello."

"You okay?"

Kelly immediately recognized the caller's voice and started coughing again. Goodness. It was Diamere. "I'm fine. Just choking on my water."

"Oh, for a moment there I thought maybe I had that type of effect on you."

She hesitated, then asked, "Who is this?"

He paused, obviously stunned by her response. Kelly chuckled inwardly. *That's what he gets for being so cocky.*

"You mean to tell me you don't know who's speaking?"

A smile touched Kelly's lips. "No," she said, and leaned back against the chocolate granite countertop. "I don't."

"Yes, you do. I can hear your smile."

She quickly forced her lips downward. "How can you hear a smile?"

"Easily. I know your voice and I know how you sound when those beautiful lips of yours are curled upward. Like right now."

"Diamere, you think you know me."

He chuckled. "I know you quite well. Just like I know you were pretending not to know it was me on the phone. But I forgive you."

"Thanks…I think," she replied with a giggle.

"You're quite welcome. Although, for giving me such a hard time, I think you now owe me."

"Owe you?" she repeated.

"Yep. You owe me a big favor. Actually, it's for my nana."

Oh, boy. He wasn't playing fair. Over the years Kelly had learned that he and his grandmother were extremely close. "What does your grandmother need?"

"The retirement center where she lives needs volunteers to help with their annual dance."

"That sounds simple enough. What would I have to do?"

"Just look beautiful and make sure the residents are having a good time," Diamere began in a low, composed tone. "Especially the male residents. Some of them haven't seen a beautiful woman like you in a long while."

Kelly couldn't stop smiling. "So my job is to entertain little old men?"

"Yep. I think you'll make quite a few of them very happy."

His words caused her heart to flutter.

"So, can I depend on your help?" he pressed.

How in the world could she say no to an event that benefited the elderly? "Sure. I'd be glad to lend a hand."

"Thanks. Nana will appreciate it." There was a noticeable pause. "So, are we on for this Friday?"

"Yes, unless you've changed your mind."

"No. I'm looking forward to it."

She smiled. "So am I."

"Well, I'll see you then, Kellis Michele Saunders."

"You, too, Diamere Travis Redmond."

Hanging up the receiver, Kelly returned to her bedroom, retrieved Devin's card and tossed it into the trash.

Chapter 7

"I heard through the grapevine you've got a date tomorrow?"

Glancing up from her desk, Kelly spotted Essence sashaying into her classroom, eyes dancing with mischief. Kelly playfully rolled her eyes and lowered her pen. "I don't even need to guess who's been running his mouth."

Essence laughed and leaned back, resting her weight against a student's desk in the front row. "And I suppose you weren't going to tell me." She even had the nerve to look offended. Kelly knew her well enough not to fall for that.

She wagged her index finger. "I knew if I told you you'd run and blab your mouth, but I guess it didn't matter, since Diamere ran his own mouth." Leaning back in her chair, she frowned. "I don't know if I want to go out with someone who gossips."

"Girl, puhleeze! That man is just excited is all. When I asked him about lunch the other day, he…" Realizing she had just told on herself, Essence trailed off.

Kelly pursed her lips. "Now I see how it is."

"I just wanted to know how lunch went," she admitted sheepishly.

"You could have asked me," Kelly said in a quiet voice.

"Yeah…or I could go straight to the source. Diamere came over last night and I asked him when Mark wasn't in the room."

Curiosity got the best of Kelly. "Well, quit beating around the bush and tell me."

The corners of Essence's mouth inched higher. "Now who's being nosy?" When she saw the impatient look on her friend's face she said, "Okay, okay. Diamere said he had never wanted anything as much as he wanted a second chance with you."

Her heart skipped a beat. "You're kidding."

Essence shook her head. "Nope. He did."

A second chance? Was that what was happening between them? Oh, how often she had wished, dreamed and hoped that she would have the chance to start where they left off. But too many years had passed. And it was too late for second chances. So what was happening between them? *Absolutely nothing,* Kelly told herself, then pushed aside the feelings that were fluttering at her chest. She was just trying to find a way to get Diamere out of her system once and for all. After Devin, love was the last thing she needed.

"We're going to have dinner and see a movie. That's all. Just two friends catching up."

"You keep telling yourself that and maybe you'll start believing it."

Kelly shot her a warning look. "Don't you have some lesson plans to prepare?"

Essence stood and glanced over at the clock. "All done. And it's noon, so I think it's time to go shopping."

Kelly's brow rose. "Shopping? What are you buying now?" Everyone knew Essence was a shopaholic.

Resting her hands on her narrow hips, she smiled down at Kelly. "Not me. You. We're going to lunch and then we're going to find you something sexy to wear for tomorrow night."

Kelly groaned. Essence was not going to give up until she agreed. Reluctantly, she closed her lesson plan and reached for her purse. She might as well eat something first, because she was in for a long afternoon.

Just as Kelly suspected, it was almost six when she finally stepped through her front door. Without bothering to look at the mail, she moved down the hall to her bedroom with her arms filled with bags. As soon as she neared the bed, she lowered them to the floor and fell back onto the mattress with a heavy sigh. She had always loved to shop, but nothing could have prepared her for the marathon Essence had run her through. They had gone through every department store in the mall. Lingerie, shoes, jewelry and clothing. Kelly had to admit she'd enjoyed herself, but she wasn't ready to repeat that adventure for a long time.

Anxious to see the items she'd allowed Essence to con her into buying, she sat up on her bed, reached for a small red-and-pink bag and removed a red demi bra and matching low-rise panties. *Sexy.* Her lips curled upward. Just having the satin material against her skin made her feel seductive and in total control. Diamere wouldn't get the chance to see her in them, but at least she could feel naughty with her own little secret.

From the next box she pulled out a little black dress with a low-cut front. That was one outfit she would never have considered buying, but Essence had insisted she try it on. Kelly was reluctant at first, but once she did she knew there was no way she was leaving without it. It hugged every curve and made her feel sexier than she ever had.

Next she pulled out a black box and removed a pair of black patent leather stiletto sandals. Slipping off her mules, she slid her feet into the shoes, strapped them on and strutted across the room in front of the mirror near her closet door. Working as a schoolteacher, she usually wore low heels so she'd be comfortable all day. On weekends she rarely wore heels except for special occasions. She paused and stared at her reflection as she tried to figure out what made this date more exciting than the one she'd had two months ago, with a neighbor's son her mother had tried fixing her up with. *It wasn't with Diamere.*

Just thinking about him seeing her in the outfit and stilettos made her heart pitter-patter. She was looking forward to tomorrow night even if she didn't care to admit it.

Staring at her reflection, Kelly took a moment to note how flushed her cheeks were at the thought of spending an entire evening with Diamere. She drew a deep breath and forced herself to relax. She couldn't afford to lose her head.

One thing she had to remember was that no matter

how much fun she had tomorrow, no matter how much her pulse raced, it was just a date between friends, nothing more. So why wasn't her heart listening?

Chapter 8

On Friday, Kelly hurried home from school and spent the rest of the afternoon getting ready for her date with Diamere. She was a nervous wreck and thought a hot bath was just what she needed to calm her nerves. She was a grown woman and yet her heart fluttered with anticipation. After adjusting the water temperature, she reached for the mango-scented bubble bath and poured a capful under the faucet. The steamy heat would totally relax her and she needed that.

The doorbell rang. Kelly frowned, wondering who could possibly be visiting. Quickly, she slipped on a robe and hurried down the hall. She opened the door to find a flower deliveryman standing outside. Her eyes grew as he handed her a large box wrapped beautifully in pink cellophane and tied with a white bow and curly streamer. She couldn't believe Devin. He'd been sending her gifts since she left Texas. She regretted leaving a forwarding address at her former school. Kelly was tempted to tell the deliveryman to take the box and give it to his girlfriend. But, plastering on a smile, she thanked him and closed the door.

Kelly carried the box to the table and reached for the card, all set to roll her eyes. Instead, she gasped when she read the inscription. "Looking forward to spending the evening with you." She laughed at herself for jumping to conclusions. The gift was from Diamere. He was definitely starting the night off on the right foot.

She opened the box and smiled. Inside were a dozen roses, one pink and eleven white. Kelly brought the pink one to her nose and inhaled. She loved roses, especially pink ones, and Diamere knew it. As she carried the box to the kitchen, she remembered how on her sixteenth birthday her father had bought her sixteen pink roses and how ecstatic she had been. Diamere had been there and her father had explained her love for the flower. She clearly recalled Diamere saying, "I'll have to remember that," and remember he did. Her smile widened. She reached under the sink, removed a glass vase and filled it with cool water before adding the beautiful arrangement.

"Oh, my God!" Kelly gasped. Leaving the vase on the kitchen counter, she scrambled down the hall and into her bedroom to find the water in the bathtub climbing dangerously close to the top. Quickly, she turned off the tap and reached for the drain, letting out just enough to allow room for her own body.

Kelly returned to her room long enough to strip off her robe, then padded naked back into the bathroom and sank into the tub of hot bubbles. With a sigh, she rested her head against the bath pillow and allowed herself to relax. All she could think about was her date tonight and it had her body humming with anticipation.

Closing her eyelids, she found images of Diamere's handsome face appearing front and center. Kelly felt her nipples begin to harden. There was no doubt about it. The coffee-brown man was fine, inside and out. Any woman who had the privilege of being in his company should feel special. And tonight she was going to be the center of his attention. Her tongue slipped from between her lips and she moistened her suddenly dry lips at the thought of spending the entire evening staring into his big beautiful eyes. After years of wishing and wondering, she was finally going out on her first real date with him. Her heart pounded heavily at the possibilities.

Kelly drew a leg to her chest and released a heavy breath. Years of heartache had taught her a painful lesson. No way was she going to make more of tonight than it truly was. However, even as that thought filled her mind, she couldn't help but think that they were both mature, and single. Both had made it clear they weren't looking for any kind of commitment. Kelly appreciated Diamere's honesty. After his marriage to Ryan, the last thing he wanted was to be tied down. That was fine with her. This way there was no misunderstanding. Whatever happened between them would never be any more than it was.

So why does that bother you?

Kelly sank lower in the tub and pushed the ridiculous thought aside. The last thing she wanted was a relationship, even one with a man she had spent so many years secretly longing for. All she had time for in her life was her students and her studies. She was one semester away from graduation. It had been a long, difficult road, juggling a full-time teaching position and attending classes in the evening, but soon her hard work would finally pay off. Although she loved teaching, Kelly hoped by applying for the assistant principal position she would have more time to spend with the children and their parents. She was a strong believer that communication and patience were the keys to a child's future.

Reaching for her washcloth, Kelly lathered it and rubbed it across her arm. Yes, she didn't have time for a relationship, but that didn't mean she couldn't have fun. She was still a woman who was very attracted to a handsome man. What was wrong with finally finding out what she had been missing all these years? At the rate she was going she was going to die a virgin. True, she had been saving her virginity all these years for that special man in her life, but after a few too many dysfunctional relationships, and her farce of an engagement, she was starting to believe love just wasn't meant for her. So what was she supposed to do in the meantime?

As she rinsed off, Kelly made a decision. Tonight she was going to go for it. She was going to let whatever happened happen. She gave a nervous smile as her decision solidified. Her heart was pounding with fear of the unknown and anticipation of what she was about to experience. One thing was for sure. If Diamere was in the driver's seat, it would be nothing short of amazing. Tonight she would get everything she was certain only Diamere could provide, and give in to the feelings that only he knew how to satisfy. And after tonight she would move on as if nothing in her life had changed. Although Kelly had a sinking feeling that it already had.

Thirty minutes later she was in her room, slipping on her new red satin panties and matching demi bra. She loved the way the latter emphasized her ample breasts. Moving to the bed, she reached for the short black dress and pulled it over her head. Kelly looked into the full-length mirror and was just as pleased as when she'd tried it on in the store. It had been designed to draw the attention of even the least observant to the perfect lines of her figure. She rarely worked out anymore, and had the occasional eating binge, yet she still managed to keep her petite figure in shape. She smiled, thinking of her mother's warning that once Kelly had kids of her own, her hips would spread and her hearty appetite would make her start packing on the pounds. Hopefully that was a long time away.

Kelly reached for a bottle of perfume and sprayed her neck and the inside of her wrists with the clean, fresh scent. Tonight she didn't want to wear anything too strong, just something soft and subtle enough to draw Diamere's attention. Her heart fluttered at the thought of him pressing his thick, juicy lips against hers again. Kelly couldn't help but imagine him trailing a path down her chest and traveling down to her— *Enough!*

She was asking for trouble, letting her mind go there. The evening was about having fun and living for the moment, and if they ended up doing more than just kissing, so be it. But she wasn't going to initiate anything. The night would be about spontaneity.

By seven Kelly was dressed, and slid on the stilettos. Reaching for her jewelry box, she removed a pair of diamond studs that had once belonged to her mother, and stuck them in her ears. She had just finished putting on her makeup when she heard the doorbell chime.

Diamere had arrived. She felt knots in her stomach, but took two deep breaths and headed down the hall. Never before had she allowed a man to get to her like that. *He's just a man, he's just a man,* she repeated in her head. But when she swung the door open, her breath caught in her throat. Her hands began to sweat and her mouth turned dry at the sight of him. This was the same man who had been invading her dreams all week. Her eyes traveled the length of his stunning body. He was wearing khaki slacks and a pale yellow button-down shirt, but he looked sexy enough to grace a magazine cover.

"Hey, sexy." He made no attempt to disguise his appreciation for her as his gaze passed slowly over her body. The tight black dress was already serving its purpose.

Running her tongue over her lower lip, she met his eyes and smiled. "Hello," she said, her voice sounding as if it were in some far-off place. "Come on in. I'm just about ready."

Diamere watched Kelly disappear down the hall, and when she was out of sight he realized he had been holding his breath.

The dress she wore hugged every luscious curve of her petite body, while the stilettos emphasized her toned legs. As she moved away, he watched the enticing roundness of her backside and wondered how a woman that small could have that many curves. As aroused as he was, he knew he had to get his thoughts in order quickly or he was going to find himself moving down the hall and into her bedroom to take a closer look at those long legs.

Even though he wasn't interested in getting seriously involved with another woman, Diamere couldn't help feeling curious about what it would be like to be with her in every way. Last night, while he lay in bed, he wondered what would have happened if he hadn't married Ryan. He always knew that he and Kelly had a lot in common, and they were friends, which was very important. He was a strong believer that couples needed to be friends before they could ever become more serious. He was certain that if he'd had the chance back then, he and Kelly would have hit it off both in and out of the bedroom. They might have been the ones that ended up married instead of him and Ryan.

Diamere brushed his thoughts aside long enough to admire the cream walls, polished hardwood floor, cathedral ceiling and large windows of Kelly's living room. She definitely had a flair for decorating. Maybe he could convince her to come over and give him some tips. Just thinking about her coming to his condo had his mind wandering off into dangerous territory. *There's nothing wrong with enjoying each other,* he told himself. One thing he truly appreciated was that they had already put their feelings on the table and had been honest about not looking for a commitment. That was good. Real good. Because the last thing he wanted to do was hurt Kelly. He cared about her too much. Now he would be able to enjoy their time together without having to worry about any miscommunication. Because last night he had made a decision. He wasn't going to dictate the evening. He was going to allow things to flow on their own and if nothing happened, he was not going to be the least bit disappointed. After all, the night was young and anything was possible.

"I'm all set."

At the sound of her voice, Diamere swung around and found Kelly standing there with a black purse over her shoulder. She had applied soft pink lipstick, which he was already tempted to kiss off. He decided to allow her to wear it for now, but before the evening was over he planned to have her lips bare, wet and swollen. He knew once he started kissing her it was going to be next to impossible to stop.

Chapter 9

Diamere helped Kelly into his Navigator, and as soon as their seat belts were safely in place he pulled away from the curb and headed toward the highway.

"You smell good," he told her.

Kelly turned her head toward him and smiled. "Thanks. It's called Pearls. It's one of my favorite scents."

"I can see why." He gave her a smile that intensified the ache in her body.

She giggled to herself. The compliment was exactly what she had hoped for. Tonight she wanted to make sure she had his undivided attention. She had noticed his appreciative stare at the door and knew his eyes had been on her backside as she sashayed to her room to finish getting ready. Everything was going according to plan, and if things continued, before the night was over she would finally find out, after years of wishing and wondering, what it was like to be made love to by Diamere Redmond. A nervous shiver of anticipation traveled right down to her core, and she squeezed her legs tightly together.

"You okay?"

"What?" Her head snapped to the left. "I'm fine. Why do you ask?"

"Because you just moaned."

Oh, no! Did I really do that out loud? "Oh, no. I...I was humming a tune I heard earlier," she said, pleased at how fast she could think under pressure.

"Then I guess I should have asked why were you crying, because you've never been able to carry a tune."

Kelly playfully slugged him in the arm. "I can too carry a tune."

"Ow!" he cried, trying to keep the laughter out of his voice. He rubbed his arm as if she had actually hurt him. "The Kelly Saunders I remember tried to sing Mariah Carey at one of her family reunions and got gonged after the first minute."

It only took a few seconds for her to remember the exact summer he was talking about. Kelly exploded with laughter at the reminder. She had been seventeen at the time and thought she was going to be the next worldwide singing sensation. At every Saunders family reunion they held a talent night and she had been determined to show her parents how well she could sing. It wasn't long before one of her cousins tossed a deviled egg at her head.

"Okay, I have to agree I sounded awful," she said with a hearty chuckle at the memories.

"Awful? You had the neighbor's dog howling at the

moon!" Diamere tore his eyes away from the road long enough to meet her gaze, and as soon as he did they exploded with even more laughter.

"You're right. After that night I decided that maybe I better become a teacher instead."

"I think you made the right choice," he replied with a playful glint in his eyes.

Diamere maneuvered the sleek vehicle onto the highway, heading toward Philadelphia. "I hope you don't mind going to see that new horror movie. I know movies aren't considered good choices for first dates."

"You know I love a good scary movie as much as you do. Besides, that rule applies to people who are just getting to know each other. I think I already know everything I need to know about you."

Diamere glanced at her out the corner of his eye. "You think you know me, huh?"

"Of course," she replied with a playful smirk. "At least what I need to know."

Diamere focused on the road as he slowly nodded his head and said, "Okay, we'll see about that."

Kelly didn't miss the hint of a challenge in his voice, and the possibility excited her. The night was filled with possibilities.

The movie was just what she needed. They shared a bucket of popcorn, an extra-large cola and chocolate-covered raisins. By the middle of the film, Kelly was jumping out of her seat. Diamere reached over and laced his fingers with hers and she relaxed, leaning her head on his shoulder.

After the movie, Diamere took her hand as they

walked to his car side by side, neither saying anything, just enjoying the other's company.

"Anything you would like to do before we go to dinner?"

She looked up at him for a moment and then a big smile spread across her face. "How about a carriage ride? I haven't done that in years."

"Sounds like a plan."

He drove to the historical district and parked his SUV in a garage and got out. Extending a hand, he helped her down from her side.

Kelly climbed out and glanced at her feet. "I forgot to consider that these probably aren't the best walking shoes."

"I've got a solution." With that, Diamere swung her up into his arms and carried her across the parking lot while she struggled to get free.

"Diamere, put me down!" she cried as she tightened her grip on his neck.

"I'm trying to help you," he answered, ignoring her request.

Kelly felt the power of his body as he shifted her comfortably in his arms. She felt the heat emanating from him and needed some distance before she got too excited. "My feet will be fine," she protested.

Stopping, Diamere stared at her, unblinking. His mouth was only inches from hers. Desire stirred, causing her heart to pound heavily as they looked at each other, tension shimmering between them.

"If you insist." His gaze lingered on her mouth before moving up to her eyes.

"Yes, I do," she whispered.

Diamere possessed a sexy, animal-like magnetism

she had never been so conscious of before. He stared at her and she held her breath, wondering what he was planning to do next. She released it silently when he obediently lowered her to the ground.

"Trust me, women learn how to walk in stilettos." She didn't bother to tell him that women went through a lot to look good even if they got an occasional blister from it.

"I don't know how you do it, but I'd be lying if I didn't say how sexy you look in those shoes," he said.

A smile curved her mouth. "Thank you." She didn't know what it was about Diamere that made her think such wicked thoughts. She couldn't help imagining wearing those shoes to bed…his bed.

"Well, we'd better get walking."

The sound of his low voice brought her back to the present. Curving a protective arm around her waist, Diamere led her up the block to Fourth and Chestnut, where there were carriages lined up along the street.

Kelly carefully chose what she thought looked like the friendliest horse. Diamere stood by, trying to suppress his laughter. When she finally decided on a horse named Charlie, they boarded the carriage.

The temperature had dropped to about seventy-eight degrees and it was slightly humid, yet Kelly still found herself shivering from nerves and anticipation. Once they were both comfortably seated, the horse backed away from the curb and began a slow trot. Kelly glanced around. She had taken this tour in the past and loved hearing the driver narrate the history of the area.

"You look like you're enjoying yourself tonight," Diamere whispered.

She turned her head to meet his stare and her eyes

widened. She was at a loss for words. She shivered as if a cool breeze had swept the back of her neck. There was something about the way he looked at her that made her want to tell him she'd feel even better if he took her back to his condo and made love to her. A smile played at the corners of his mouth as if he knew what she was thinking. "I am having a great time," she finally answered.

He looked pleased by her response. "Good. If you weren't I'd be afraid I'm losing my touch."

She shook her head and shifted on the carriage seat. "Heaven forbid anyone would say Diamere Redmond doesn't know how to treat a lady."

He gave a hearty chuckle. "Absolutely. We definitely can't have that."

As the carriage turned onto the next street, the guide's robust voice drew their attention. Kelly only half listened. Her mind was on Diamere. She remembered he'd once had quite the reputation for being a ladies' man. That was before he finally decided to marry. Now that he was single again, she was certain it would be hard for a woman to ever penetrate the wall he'd erected after the way Ryan had betrayed him.

From the beginning he'd been up-front about not looking for anything serious. And that was a good thing, because as long as they both knew where the other stood, Kelly wouldn't be in jeopardy of losing her heart to him again. Despite knowing this, she still responded to his nearness. She shifted her weight and thought about the attraction that exploded between them each and every time she looked his way. Her pulse was racing. She didn't want to stop looking at him. In fact, she wanted him to kiss her again.

As if he knew she was watching him out of the corner of her eye, Diamere reached over and took her hand in his. A shiver of anticipation raced through her.

"Are you cold?" he asked, in a tone she found both comforting and unsettling.

She took a deep breath and finally shook her head.

Diamere studied her intently before he leaned over and whispered in her ear, "Don't worry. I don't bite."

Kelly saw the heat in his eyes, the glint of arousal. She could feel the intensity overwhelming her. *Relax,* she commanded herself.

Diamere draped an arm across her shoulders, which she found quite comforting. As the guide took them along one cobblestone street after the next, she found herself relaxing, and without realizing it nestled her head against Diamere's shoulder as they listened to the driver's narration. By the time she realized what she was doing, she had to admit it felt quite natural. Diamere was large and solid, just right for resting her head. She inhaled his masculine scent.

"Are you falling asleep?" he asked quietly.

Kelly tilted her head and looked up at him. "Of course not. I'm just listening."

A slow, sexy smile flattened his upper lip against the ridge of his teeth. "It sounded like you were snoring."

"Snoring? Diamere, quit pulling my leg!"

He barked with laughter as she playfully swatted his arm. They shared a laugh, then resumed listening to the rest of the tour so as not to be rude. As the carriage traveled along the quiet streets, Diamere continued to drape his arm across Kelly's shoulders, holding her hand and grazing his thumb across her knuckles. She felt the slow, sensual strokes clear down to her toes. When the carriage moved down South Street, the street that never sleeps, Diamere pressed his lips against the top of her head for a brief moment.

"Hey."

As her eyes locked upon his, the rest of the world seemed to fade away. "What?"

"Thanks for coming out with me tonight." Her breath caught in her chest as she remembered the last time she'd seen that strange simmering quality. It was right before he had kissed her.

"I'm having a wonderful time just being here with you," she admitted with a smile. Then, just as she'd anticipated, his head came down and his lips covered hers.

Kelly didn't resist. She gave in to temptation. There was no denying it; she had been waiting all night for this moment. Now she didn't want it to stop. Any apprehensions of where the evening might end just faded away. She wanted nothing more than for Diamere to make love to her.

As his lips parted hers, she eagerly opened her mouth. When his tongue thrust forward, she touched it with the tip of hers. All she thought about was what she felt, and what she was feeling was spontaneous and free. She felt young and new to the sensation, although she had certainly been kissed before. She felt alive in ways she hadn't in years. He finally ended the kiss, and gave her a look that said he understood exactly how she was feeling.

"I think that will last me for a little while."

He then tightened the arm around her shoulders and drew her near again. She lowered her head to his chest and her eyes slowly shut as she succumbed to his spell.

Even though she had made the decision to sleep with him, things were spiraling out of control. She was supposed to dictate the night's events, not him. She wanted to lead, to make sure her heart didn't become involved. Right now her body was throbbing so hard she could hardly think straight. They were not only sitting close and holding hands, but taking a romantic ride around the city. Inhaling deeply, she forced herself to get a grip. For the duration of the ride she tried to regain control of her emotions by taking a stab at casual conversation about their surroundings. But it didn't work. Her body and heart were at war. Finally, exactly one hour from the time they'd departed, the carriage came full circle and pulled back into its original spot.

"Stay right there," Diamere said quietly. He got down from the carriage, thanked and tipped the driver, then returned and held out his arms to her. Seconds later, Kelly jumped into them. Instead of lowering her to her feet, he held her effortlessly, her shoes dangling several inches from the ground. Her arms circled his neck as she attempted to maintain her balance. His fingers tightened around her waist, bringing her breasts into contact with the solid wall of his chest. She felt the heat of his flesh through the layers of clothing. Her head, level with his, eased forward until she felt the whisper of his moist breath as it swept over her mouth. Desire burned in his eyes.

Kelly smothered a groan. She was certain Diamere could feel her sensitive nipples hardened like tiny pebbles. Passion had her pulse pumping, and she had to struggled to maintain what little was left of her composure.

Diamere slowly lowered her to her feet. "You hungry yet?" he finally asked.

She playfully nodded her head. If he only knew how hungry she truly was, he would have scooped her into his arms and had carried her back to his SUV. She wanted him and she knew he wanted her, as well. The sooner she got him out of her system the better. But she was starting to have a sinking feeling that the evening wasn't going to be quite as simple as she had originally thought.

They walked back to the car and drove in silence the few blocks to the restaurant. As soon as they entered they were escorted to a small table close to the window. They looked over the menus and ordered quickly. After their waiter left, Kelly excused herself and disappeared into the ladies' room. She washed her hands, then looked in the mirror and took a deep breath. So far the night was everything she had hoped for. Now it was time to turn things up a notch.

The second she walked back out the door, there would be no turning back. Either she was going home with him or returning to her condo with her virginity still intact. This was her last chance to run. She gazed at the woman in front of her and knew from the color of her cheeks that she wanted nothing as much as she wanted to spend the night in Diamere's arms.

Reaching into her purse, she grabbed her compact and dusted her face with powder, then added a sheen of gloss to her lips. A smiled appeared on her lips at the thought of where she wanted the evening to end. *Too bad it's only for one night.* Thank goodness Diamere wasn't looking for anything long-term, otherwise she might find herself losing her heart to him a second time. As long as she kept reminding herself that she was living for the moment, she would be all right.

Picking up her purse, she swung the strap over her shoulder, then drew one more deep, shaky breath. It was time to put her plan into action.

Chapter 10

Diamere watched Kelly moving back toward the table in those shoes. He wasn't sure what it was, but in those few minutes she had spent in the ladies' room, something about her had changed. Maybe it was the way she held her head high or the way her hips swayed seductively as she walked toward him. It wasn't until she sat down that his eyes looked hungrily to the enticing roundness of her breasts and he realized she had loosened a button, which provided a whole lot of generous cleavage. Now he could see the tops of her breasts peeking out from beneath a lacy red bra. *Her favorite color.*

He swallowed, trying to ignore the wave of arousal that had traveled down to his loins. Thank goodness he was sitting down.

"Did you miss me?" Kelly purred.

"Yes, as a matter fact, I did."

"Good," she replied, just as the waiter returned with

their drinks. She brought the cosmopolitan to her lips. "Mmm," she moaned, then ran her tongue across her mouth.

Diamere was so turned on he decided to find a safe topic, like the weather, to talk about, then a news report on the economic conditions aired on television the night before. The conversation was boring, and no matter how hard he tried to repress them, thoughts of making love to Kelly kept creeping through his mind. By the time they finished dinner he was dying to throw her over his shoulder, carry her back to his car and drive her to his condo as fast as he could without getting a speeding ticket. Every time she looked at him, desire engulfed him. Diamere shifted in his chair, his arousal pressed painfully against the front of his slacks.

Their waiter returned with their dessert and Diamere dragged his eyes from Kelly, trying to concentrate on the strawberry shortcake in front of him. He brought a bite to his lips and was pleased to find it was delicious. The strawberries were red and ripe and the cream was fresh.

Kelly pierced a berry with her fork, then slowly slid the fruit between her lips. "Mmm," she moaned, then licked off the drop of cream that clung to her bottom lip.

Diamere's fork paused in midair.

Slowly, she brought the fork to her lips again, but this time licked the cream from the utensil with her gaze locked with his. The attraction he'd been fighting suddenly blazed into a roaring California wildfire. Diamere dropped his fork to the table and raised his hand to signal their waiter. "We're ready for the check."

Eyes wide with innocence, Kelly looked at him with

confusion. "What are you talking about? I haven't had my coffee yet."

"I'll buy you a cup later. Hell, I'll buy you your own coffeemaker." No sooner had the waiter arrived with the check than Diamere tossed a stack of bills on the table and rose from his chair. "Thank you for your service." He hooked Kelly by the arm and led her quickly out the restaurant.

"What in the world has gotten into you?" she asked as he practically dragged her down the street.

"I can show you better than I can tell you." And he planned to do just that as soon he got her to his condo and into his bed.

"Would you please slow down! I can't keep up in these shoes."

When they reached the corner, Diamere stopped, swept her up into his arms and carried her down the street. Kelly gasped and looped her arms around his neck to steady herself. "You are being ridiculous."

"Sweetheart, you haven't seen anything yet," he said quietly.

"What is wrong with you?"

"I think you know. If you don't, I'll be happy to show you as soon as we get to my place."

Kelly tightened her hold on Diamere's neck as he carried into his condo. "You can put me down now."

"Not yet."

She didn't even have a chance to look around and appreciate his place. With long strides he moved through the condo and down the hall. As soon as he reached his bedroom, he lowered her to her feet, then bent his head and covered her lips with his.

Dear God, I have unleashed a monster, she thought. Diamere had every intention of taking her tonight whether she liked it or not. She began to grow nervous as she wondered if maybe this was as good a time as any to let him know she was still a virgin. Only, she couldn't think with his body pressed so close to hers and his lips devouring her. She could barely take a breath before he pushed her lips apart and swept his tongue inside. Heat was rushing through her so fast her head was spinning.

He placed a finger under her chin and tilted her face so she had no choice but to look at him. When Diamere finally spoke, his voice was low and controlled. "If you are having any doubts, tell me now, because once I start I don't know if I'll be able to stop." For a long, endless moment, he held her with his eyes. "I've waited for this for a long time. A long, long time," he repeated softly. He lowered his head and brushed his mouth against hers once more before he pulled back and looked at her again. "Do you want me?" he asked. His fingers slid across her cheek, then cupped the back of her head, and once again he lowered his mouth to hers.

She couldn't speak, couldn't move. She could only stand there while he kissed her, opening her mouth and letting his tongue explore every corner of it. It seemed to her that his kiss lasted both forever and yet for the briefest moment.

Diamere paused. "Tell me you want me," he commanded in a soft, low voice.

Reaching up, Kelly stroked his face with the tips of

her fingers, running them across his cheek, jaw and his strong neck. "I want you," she breathed.

He smiled. "And I want you." He carried her over to the bed and lowered her onto it. It was massive and plush, with a comforter so thick she felt as if she had stepped inside heaven.

He looked down at her, lying there on the huge bed. "You're so beautiful," he said softly.

Her eyes rested on Diamere as he undid the buttons of his shirt. She could only watch as he pulled the shirt off and tossed it onto an upholstered chair in the corner. Her eyes lingered on his beautiful lean chest, which was nothing short of perfect. She was dying to run her fingers across his nipples, and was certain that, before the night was over, she would. Mesmerized by what was about to happen, Kelly could not move. She knew she needed to tell him the truth before it was too late, but she couldn't do anything except lie there and watch as Diamere removed the rest of his clothes.

The entire time, he looked down at her, his gaze holding her immobilized. He unbuckled his belt, then unzipped his pants, and they fell to the floor, followed by his boxers. Panic caused her eyes to widen at the sight of him. He was large. So large her pulse raced. There was no way a woman could accommodate such a man. Yet, despite her fear, her body began to hum with a need she didn't understand.

Naked, Diamere lowered himself onto the bed beside her and carefully loosened the buttons of her dress, finally pulling it over her head with slow deliberation. He reached behind her, unsnapped her bra and tossed it aside, freeing her breasts. Kelly swallowed and they peaked beneath his gaze, and for one painfully long moment she simply stared at him, letting him look at her. Then, exhaling with a sigh, she murmured, "Diamere, I need to tell…" Her voice trailed off as his lips closed around a nipple. "Diamere…" Again she gave a blissful sigh.

His lips were like nothing she had ever felt. Although she was still a virgin, she'd had moments where kissing had led to serious petting and touching, forms of foreplay that she always stopped before things got out of hand. But that didn't compare to what he was doing to her. *This* was what making love was truly all about. She needed him. She didn't care if it was only one night; it didn't matter if she might have regrets tomorrow. All she knew was that this was the moment she had been waiting for all her life.

His lips traveled downward to her belly, and not long after that he slipped her panties down her hips, and she heard the sound of him ripping open what must be a condom. Nervousness pounded through her, but quickly subsided when he kissed her again as his body covered hers.

"I can't wait any longer. I've got to have you." With a soft growl of need, Diamere positioned himself between her trembling thighs, and in one smooth motion entered her. Feeling the strong, swift thrust of his body into hers, Kelly cried out in pain, and Diamere paused.

"Please don't stop," she protested, almost pleading, when he remained motionless.

Raising himself up on his arms, he looked down at her for the longest time with concern in his eyes. He knew what had happened. Just when she thought he was about to refuse, he leaned down and his mouth devoured hers, hungrily, heatedly. Now that he knew her secret, she was confident he would be gentle and take his time with her.

He caressed her with tender hands and melting lips, and as her body began to relax, he reentered her slowly. Sweet desire tore through her as he established a rhythm for them. It wasn't long before her muscles responded and the tightness ceased, and she felt nothing but pleasure from every stroke of his body inside hers. And the sweetest bliss of all was the knowledge that she finally knew what it was like to be with a man. What it was like to make love to Diamere.

It was sweet and unbearable, pleasure and pain all rolled up in one, with him lying on top of her, his body sliding inside, filling every inch of her, setting her soul on fire. Kelly's mouth clung to Diamere's. Her arms were wrapped around him, holding him close as he fed her hunger, and yet it wasn't tight enough. This was what she had waited all these years to experience. She also knew it wouldn't have been this way with anyone else but him, because their connection ran deeper than anything she felt for any other man.

Diamere's strokes were slow and controlled. Withdrawing, thrusting and withdrawing again. Flames moved through her veins and something she couldn't even begin to describe began to build. She was so close to the edge. Her body tightened around him. Diamere lengthened his strokes and Kelly found that her body knew more about what was happening to her than she did. On their own, her hips began to rock, meeting him stroke for blissful stroke. Even her hands had a mind of their own as they gripped his backside, shortening his strokes, pulling him in even deeper. All she knew was that she needed desperately to feel everything Diamere Redmond had to offer.

"You like this?" he asked.

She barely had a chance to murmur yes before he began moving his body again, only this time with more powerful strokes, and with every trust, she felt that unfamiliar sensation that lit her body like a torch.

"Diamere…" Her moan was breathless, as if she was begging him never to stop.

He lifted his head and gazed down at her. She stared up at him, admiring the shadows that danced across his face from the moonlight shining through the window. Her heart flipped. Diamere was making sweet love to her now.

"Diamere," she breathed again.

"I'm right here, sweetheart," he whispered against her lips. "I'm not going anywhere."

He began to lengthen his strokes again and she arched her body to his. Time seemed to stand still. All she could see was the passion burning in his eyes. Still slow and controlled, his strokes deepened within her even more and she rocked her hips and thrashed her head against her pillow.

Heat spread through her body and she cried out as sensations raged, like nothing she'd ever felt before. Diamere continued to move, controlled yet urgent, and the unstoppable stimulation went on and on until he finally cried out, as well. She clung to him as she felt his body convulse into hers. She moaned audibly until, with one final pulse, he sighed, and suddenly the weight of his exhausted body was lying on top of her.

As soon as his breathing stilled, he raised up on his elbows and stared down at her. Her heart was pounding, her body shaken over what she had just experienced. She waited for what felt like forever before he finally spoke.

"Did I hurt you?" he asked, his expression filled with concern.

Hurt was definitely not one of the things she was feeling. The only thing in jeopardy of being hurt was her heart. "No."

"Why didn't you tell me?"

She met his eyes. "Would you have changed your mind if you had?"

He took a moment to consider his answer. "No. I've wanted that for a long time. But if I knew, I would have taken more time and been more gentle."

"You didn't hurt me. I wanted it."

He kissed her lips and asked, "Why me?"

Briefly, she lowered her eyelids and blew out a long breath. "I was tired of being a virgin, and if I did it with anyone, I'm glad it was with you. I know you and I trust you." She wanted to say, *It was my gift to you. Because I saved my virginity for the man I love.* As much as she didn't want it to be true, she had fallen in love with Diamere for the second time. A part of her believed that she had never stopped loving him. The realization that she still loved him caused her to choke back a sob. *No. This is not happening.*

"Thank you for giving me the honor." He brushed his lips against her nose and cheek. "Am I too heavy?"

"No," she whispered. The only thing heavy was her heart.

Diamere stared at her a few seconds longer. His look shook her to her core. He lowered his head and pressed his lips against hers, then feathered kisses across her face. With a deep sigh, he moved onto the bed beside her, then rested his head against the crook of her neck and within seconds drifted off to sleep.

Kelly lay there wrapped in the comfort of his warm body nestled beside her. For the longest time she simply listened to his deep breathing. *I could get used to this.* And that was a problem. Diamere had finally made love to her. She had given him her virginity, he had taken her to a place she had dreamed about going with him for years, and now, as she lay there in his bed, she was ready for him to make love to her again. Kelly frowned. Things were not going at all the way she had planned. The purpose of them making love was so she would be rid of her virginity and finally be able to close that chapter in her life. As soon as she had a nap she was going to insist that Diamere take her home.

Feeling more at ease, she closed her eyes and snuggled close to him.

"What are you thinking about?" he asked, breaking into her thoughts.

She buried her head against his shoulder. "Nothing. I thought you were asleep."

His arms tightened around her. "Nope. I'm not sleepy. Just thinking," he whispered close to her ear.

"What are you thinking about?" she dared to ask.

He leaned over and very softly kissed her. "You."

Diamere's words and the warmth of his smile nearly made her lose control. "What about me?" Kelly turned on her side and looked at him.

"How beautiful you are. How good we are together." Oh, how she wished that were true. Diamere covered her with his warm body again and gazed down at her. "I can think of a way to put you to sleep."

She looked up at him, eyes half-closed, and smiled. "I bet you can show me better than you can tell me." She slid her arms around his neck as Diamere leaned down and kissed her. He had the sweetest, softest lips. She opened her mouth for him and felt his body harden. Within minutes he was inside her once more, the two of them moving in perfect rhythm. They reached their release together, a fierce climax that had them both crying out with the greatest pleasure. As she lay there curled against his side afterward, she listened as his breathing deepened, and together they drifted into an exhausted sleep.

Chapter 11

Diamere opened his eyes and blinked several times before he realized it was morning. As soon as he noticed his crumpled shirt flung over a chair in the corner, visions of the night before flooded his mind. He rolled onto his back and lay there with a smile curled on his lips as he relived the night the two of them had had. One word immediately came to mind. *Explosive.* It certainly was, to say the least. Not to mention *intense.* Those were two things he hadn't had in a long, long time.

And you've never been with a virgin.

Diamere sucked in a deep breath. A virgin. It was still hard to believe that Kelly had held on to her virginity all these years and had given him the honor. A warm feeling curled in the pit of his stomach at the thought of her gesture. A part of him wished she had confided in him, so he would have been prepared to take things slow and gentle. But he couldn't help but wonder if he would have changed his mind if he had known. Then he lowered his eyelids and visions of her lying on his bed flooded his mind, and he knew without a doubt that nothing would have stopped him from having her. Giving him her virginity made what they had shared that much more incredible. Her gift meant more to him than she would ever know. And for some odd reason he now felt as if Kelly belonged to him. He shook off the thought and stretched his arms above his head.

Last night was supposed to be about sharing the moment, but he discovered that nothing involving Kelly was that simple. He had wanted her from the moment he had first laid eyes on her at the nightclub. He wasn't sure when he'd last woken up after making love to a woman and felt this good.

He couldn't help but wonder if he had been a little too rough. Maybe this morning he would suggest she take a long, hot soak in the tub. Last night had been Kelly's first experience, and Diamere knew he should have given her time to adjust to being with a man. But after round one, just lying next to her luscious body, he couldn't resist the strong desire to be buried inside her again. *And again,* he thought as he remembered making love with her a third time just as the sun began to rise. Blood flowing to his lower regions signaled he was more than willing for a little appetizer before breakfast. But he was being selfish. After their intense lovemaking he would have to allow her time to adjust.

He felt the space beside him and it was still warm. Kelly hadn't been gone long.

Diamere took a deep breath and tried to stay in control. He hadn't felt like this in years and yet somehow, in the course of a night, that little lady had gotten under his skin. She brought out a side of him that he hadn't known still existed. Never before had something felt so right. And he wasn't ready for it to end. The thought of spending the rest of the weekend with Kelly, lying in bed, was too tempting an opportunity to pass up.

Diamere dragged a hand across his face as he tried to convince himself it was nothing. As long as they both understood there were no emotional attachments or regrets, then what was the harm of continuing to see each other until one or the other decided they were ready for their arrangement to end? He smiled, feeling pleased with this plan. The idea was perfect.

Anxious to talk to Kelly about his proposal, Diamere flung off the sheet and rose. Moving to the dresser, he reached for a pair of shorts, slipped them on and went down the hall. When he found Kelly sitting at the kitchen table, he stopped in his tracks.

The look on Diamere's face said he wasn't expecting her to be dressed. Kelly took a sip from her mug and tried not to notice how good he looked standing in the doorway with his chest bare. Diamere's shorts hung low on his hips and her traitorous eyes followed the sprinkle of hair that traveled down his abdomen and disappeared beneath the elastic band there. Feeling the temperature suddenly rising in the room, she took another sip of her coffee and resisted the urge to fan herself. If Diamere asked, she wouldn't hesitate to pull off her clothes and drag him back to bed. After one night she was a wanton woman. One thing was for sure, she now knew what the word *horny* meant.

Kelly pulled her eyes from Diamere's naked chest

and focused on the frown on his face. "Good morning. I made coffee."

He pushed himself away from the door and his smile slowly reemerged. "How about I make us breakfast in bed?"

If the circumstances were different, she might have reconsidered. Lowering her eyes, she focused on her mug as she spoke, not trusting herself to look at him. "Oh, no. I shouldn't. I've got a million things to do this morning. So as soon as you're dressed, I'll be ready to head home." Kelly didn't have a thing planned today except to repot a couple of plants. But the sooner she put some distance between them the better. Being around Diamere was hazardous to her heart. Rising, she moved to the sink and rinsed out her cup.

"Is something wrong?"

Kelly looked over her shoulder and noted the confusion in Diamere's eyes. *Yes, there's something wrong. I'm still in love with you.* "No, why would you think that?"

He stared at her for a long moment and she felt her body quiver before he nodded and said, "Just give me a few minutes and I'll be ready to go." With that he headed to the coffeepot and poured himself a cup, then turned and walked back down the hall to his room.

After he was gone, Kelly leaned against the counter and tried to pull herself together. *This is not going to be easy.* The look of disappointment in his eyes was proof of that. Last night had been a mistake. She knew that the moment she woke up and found herself lying in his bed with no desire to leave. She had felt totally at ease while there, as if lying in Diamere's arms was the most natural thing to do. She could have easily stayed there all morning and waited for him to waken, but if she had she might not have moved all weekend. Even now, if Diamere returned to the kitchen and asked her to stay, she would willingly succumb. Goodness, it was amazing how all of a sudden she had needs and only Diamere could meet them.

It wasn't supposed to be this way. Last night had been all about finally finding out what it was like to be with Diamere. Getting him out of her system and discovering the man she once loved had been nothing more than a childhood fantasy, with no substance at all. There had been men in her past she had truly liked, and only after a few dates had she discovered the relationship was not all it had been cracked up to be. But this…this had been different. Sex had only reinforced what she had known all alone—Diamere was her soul mate. No, this was not at all the way it was supposed to be. She wanted to be able to close this chapter of her life and move on, and not spend the rest of her life wondering *what if.* Instead, she had fallen in love again.

Kelly returned to her seat. She rested her elbow on the table and placed her chin in the palm of her hand. A feeling of dread settled in the pit of her stomach at the thought of never seeing Diamere again. Was she really having second thoughts? Did she really want more? Deep down she did, but there was no way she was going to allow herself to explore that option. Ending the relationship was the right thing, she was certain. Diamere had made it clear he wasn't looking for anything serious, and the last thing he needed was a woman falling in love with him. As much as she wished things could be different, they couldn't.

"All set if you are."

At the sound of his voice, Kelly pushed those ridiculous thoughts of forever aside and gazed at the man in question, standing in the doorway in jeans and a T-shirt, with car keys in his hand.

"Let me get my purse and we can go."

The drive back to Delaware was relatively quiet. She was grateful that the stereo was on and Lyfe was singing about change. Something had definitely changed in her life and she wasn't even thinking about her virginity.

Diamere pulled up in front of her building and put the car in Park, but left the motor running, making it clear he had no intention of coming in.

"When can I see you again?" His question took her by surprise.

Kelly turned on the seat, looked up into his dark eyes, and felt her resistance waiver. She hesitated for a moment before saying, "I think it's best if we *don't* see each other again."

"Why?"

Sadly, she shook her head. "It wouldn't work between us," she finally said.

"I think we did just fine last night." He was stating the obvious.

Kelly decided to lay her cards on the table. "That's the problem. For years I wanted nothing more than to be with you. For all these years I've been wondering what if things had been different. I thought if I could get involved in a short fling with you, find out what it was like to be in your arms, to be made love to—" she paused to swallow "—that I could finally get you out of my system. But now I know that isn't the case. Once was not enough."

Her confession made him smile. "Then what's the

problem? I'm not ready for it to end, either. I enjoyed making love to you."

She shook her head. "I just don't think I can do it. I've never been the type of woman to lead a man on."

Diamere nodded. "That much is obvious."

Kelly saw his smile and frowned. "Look, I've got so much going on in my life right now and I just don't need the complications of a relationship of any kind."

"So then you *have* gotten me out of your system?"

She looked into his eyes and saw the heat and the desire in them. She felt a pull in her chest.

"Because I can honestly say I haven't gotten you out of mine," he added, being just as open and up-front as she was. "In fact, I want you right now. I want to take you inside and taste you everywhere, starting at your feet and working my way up to all the delicious curves of your body. After I'm done I plan to make love to you for the rest of the day and late into the evening, until we fall asleep in each other's arms."

His response was not at all what she had expected. The words and the soft bass of his voice caused her body to quiver and ache down below. She had played with fire and the last thing she needed was to get burned. Diamere was only talking about a no-strings-attached sexual relationship. Nowhere in his confession did he hint at anything long-term. There was no way her heart could bear it. Kelly took a deep breath, trying to regain control. If she stayed in the SUV too much longer she might do something stupid like invite him inside.

Sensing her hesitation, Diamere leaned over and captured her mouth with his, then gently inserted his tongue and deepened the kiss. She was a willing participant. Diamere had a power over her that she couldn't explain. But Kelly knew getting involved with him would take more than she had to offer, and she couldn't let that happen. She couldn't let love and a childhood crush control her. She couldn't let the way he'd made her feel last night dictate her actions. Her relationship with Devin had been nothing like this, or she would have given him her virginity a long time ago. Diamere made her long for things she wasn't ready for—love and marriage. The two things she had put on the back burner. The two things she was unable to offer anyone right now.

With a deep, tormented moan, Kelly broke off the kiss and breathed. Diamere had a way of making her forget something as simple as filling her lungs with air. Taking another deep breath, she reached for her purse and opened the passenger door. "Thanks for a fabulous evening," she said. Then, without another word, she climbed out of the car and headed toward her condo.

Chapter 12

"Kelly."

Her attention was pulled back to her left. "What?"

"You've been here for over an hour and you haven't heard a word I said."

Kelly watched her mother at the stove, preparing Sunday dinner. It was only the two of them, but as usual she was cooking enough to feed the neighbors. "I'm fine. I was just thinking about something."

Dorlinda Saunders continued to stir the pot of chicken and dumplings while she stared at her youngest child out of the corner of her eye. "Care to share?"

Turning in her seat, Kelly looked out the window. She didn't know where to begin. She didn't know how much she wanted to admit. "Not really."

Dorlinda sucked her front teeth. "I don't know why you kids think just because I'm your mother I won't understand."

"It's nothing like that," Kelly began as she reached for a butter knife and dipped it into a bowl of homemade icing. "I was just thinking about something."

"Something, or someone?"

Kelly's head snapped around to find her mother's warm chestnut eyes looking at her inquisitively. She never had been any good at keeping things from her mom. Dropping her eyes, she spread the icing across the two layers of yellow cake before finally saying, "Did you know Diamere was back in Philadelphia?"

Her mother gave a knowing smile, then reached for an oven mitt and removed a pan of homemade rolls. "Yes, Lauren mentioned that he was living here again." She shook her head. "It's such a shame what happened with him and his wife. He adored those girls." At the disapproving look on her mother's face, Kelly could tell that Lauren Redmond, Diamere's mother, had shared every embarrassing detail. The women had been friends for years, and the way they gossiped on the phone, Kelly wasn't surprised her mother had heard about the terrible divorce. Her heart went out to Diamere. There were so many men who didn't want to be fathers, and here was a guy who wanted more than anything to be with his girls, and the privilege had been taken away from him.

"I'm sure he'll find a new girlfriend in no time," her mother replied, breaking into her thoughts.

Kelly felt a wave of jealousy at the idea of Diamere being with another woman, doing the things he had done with her to someone else. She tried to shake off the thought. He wasn't hers. She had no right thinking that way. She had no business falling in love. Kelly let out a long, shaky breath. It wasn't as if she'd tried to fall in love with him again, but there was something about

Diamere she couldn't resist. That's why she'd ended things when she had. No matter how much she missed him, ending the relationship had been for the best. If she had continued it, she would have wanted to be with him all the time. She wouldn't have given any thought to her thesis or the upcoming school year. Her only thoughts would have been about lying in Diamere's arms and staring up at his handsome face. Yep. Getting involved with him would have been a terrible mistake. She just wished her heart knew that, as well.

"I'm sure he'll find someone," Kelly finally said in a composed voice, pushing the thought aside immediately. While she finished smoothing the icing over the cake, she tried to stop thinking about Diamere, but was unsuccessful.

It had been a week since he had dropped her off at home, yet she still couldn't get their passionate night out of her mind. All she could think about was Diamere whispering in her ear while he moved slowly between her thighs, making her feel things she had no right to remember, yet couldn't forget. Every night she lay awake thinking, wanting and needing him. Every afternoon she found herself hoping she'd find him leaning against her car, offering to take her to lunch. But each day passed with no phone calls, no surprise appearances. It was as if the night they shared had never happened. If it wasn't for the movie ticket stub she found tucked in her pocket, she would have thought that maybe she had imagined the entire evening. Afraid of being rejected by another man, she didn't dare call him or even bring herself to ask Essence if she had seen him.

Every morning at school, her nosy sister-in-law had been trying to wiggle information out of her about their date, but at the moment Kelly wasn't ready to gossip. What she and Diamere had shared was too precious to tell anyone. It was one night she would always hold close to her heart.

"Why don't you ask Diamere out? He could probably use a friend." Her mother's voice brought her back to the present.

"We went out last week."

A smile was on her lips. "I'm sure you both had a lovely time."

What in the world would her mother think if she found out Kelly had not only gone out with Diamere, but given him her virginity, as well?

"I spoke to Calaine last night. She and David are planning to come up for Thanksgiving."

Kelly released a sigh of relief, grateful that her mother had finally changed the subject. "That's wonderful."

Calaine was the big sister Kelly never knew she had until she was already in her twenties. It was then that her mother had sat her down and told her a very painful story.

Dorlinda had gotten pregnant while in nursing school. As a struggling student with no family support, she had little choice but to give her baby up for adoption. It wasn't until Calaine went in search of her mother that the two were reunited. Ever since, the family had been very close. Calaine was married to David Soul and lived in Columbia, Missouri, with their three children.

Gazing out the window again, Kelly released a heavy sigh. For years she had wanted the same thing that her sister and brother had—love and marriage. But over the years she had begun to accept that maybe it just wasn't meant for her. She had believed in love when she'd first started dating Devin, and her heart had been broken. There was no way she could allow herself to go through that pain again. Down deep, she knew that the pain would be even worse with Diamere if she allowed it to happen. She loved him, there was no denying that. Yet as much as she missed him, Kelly knew she had made the right decision to end their relationship.

Chapter 13

Diamere looked down at his watch for the umpteenth time and scowled. The August dance had started well over an hour ago. It was probably smart at this point to assume Kelly wasn't coming. He tried to ignore the wave of disappointment as he glanced around at all the residents of Shady Acres. Everyone was having a good time laughing and eating in the beautifully decorated recreation room, except for him. Reaching for a ladle, he poured himself a cup of fruit punch and brought it to his lips. The cool beverage quenched his thirst. It was going to be a lot harder to quench something else. Kelly had gotten to him.

Diamere didn't know how or when it had happened but the little woman had somehow wiggled her way into his head and was seriously challenging his heart. He refused to believe it was happening and would fight it all the way, since he didn't want to fall for a woman.

The last thing he was looking for was that. However, he couldn't deny that he wanted to be with her. He missed her. Kelly lit a fire within his soul. Making love to her had been an experience like no other. He had been her first, and until he was done with her he wanted to be her only. He had an overwhelming desire to claim her as his…temporarily. He wasn't even going to entertain the idea of them having anything more than that. No matter how much he wanted her, he wasn't going to make the relationship more than it was.

Frustrated, Diamere ran a hand across his head. He had never behaved this way with a woman before— thinking about her day and night, wondering what she was doing, if she was missing him. For the past two weeks he'd lain in bed hard as a rock, with the scent of Kelly still lingering in his room. It was insane. He could have easily called another woman to come over and satisfy his needs, but right now he didn't want anyone but Kelly. His pulse began escalating from the direction his thoughts were taking.

His stubborn pride kept him from calling when he so desperately wanted to hear her soft voice. But Kelly had put the brakes on after one night, and for the life of him he couldn't figure out why. Especially when he thought the two of them had been fabulous together. He'd thought they had a mutual understanding that worked for the both of them. So why after one night, after one beautiful night, was she not at all interested in continuing their fling? He had hoped it would have lasted at least the duration of the summer. But Diamere had a strong feeling that one month or even two would not be near enough. His gut told him that Kelly was just as attracted to him as he was to her. So if that was true, why wasn't she here?

Diamere decided he wasn't doing anything but driving himself crazy. He finished the punch, tossed the cup in the trash and walked around the ballroom. Frank Sinatra was playing from the jukebox in the corner and several couples were moving around on the dance floor.

"Well, it's been an hour. I thought you were bringing a date?"

He turned and glanced down at his grandmother. Nana didn't let her five-foot stature stop her from showing him who was boss.

"I guess I got stood up," Diamere said with a shrug.

Vertical lines appeared between her hazel eyes. "Humph. Men back in my day picked you up at your home."

"I offered," he said defensively. "She had something to do and said it would be more convenient if she met me here."

Nana gave a heavy sigh. "I guess that means you're not serious with this one, either."

Oh, he was definitely serious. He just wasn't ready yet to admit just how much. "Kelly is a very special woman."

She must have seen something in his eyes because her face suddenly lit up. "Well then, go call her while I run over and dance with Neal." She giggled like a schoolgirl as she glanced across the room at a man in his eighties, sitting on a chair, sipping punch. "He's been waiting all night." She fluffed her hair. "I guess I better go put him out of his misery."

Chuckling, Diamere watched his grandmother sway

her narrow hips as she moved across the room and pulled Neal out onto the dance floor. The little lady was definitely something else.

He watched the couple dance until the hairs at the back of his neck stood up on alert. Curious about what was happening, he glanced around the room and could barely catch his breath when he spotted Kelly walking through the door. For the longest time, she stood still and looked around. Diamere stared at her for a moment, realizing just how much he'd missed her over the last week. Slowly, his eyes traveled up and down her body. His admiring gaze lingered on her long, shapely legs below the hem of a short, slim skirt. In a white blouse and two-inch heels, she looked as sexy as he'd ever seen her. He couldn't help thinking she was even more beautiful than he remembered. Kelly glanced to her right, looking over at him as he stared back at her. Raising her hand, she waved, smiling when he returned it.

Quickly, Diamere moved toward her, covering the distance in a few long strides. He hauled her up and straight into his arms as he lowered his mouth and kissed her once, twice, three times. Finally, in need of oxygen, he pulled back.

"Wow!" she said.

He smiled and her response was automatic—that lovely, lovely smile that filled his dreams.

Diamere tilted his head, eyeing the fuchsia color covering her sensual mouth. "I was hoping you were going to come."

"I'm a woman of my word," Kelly replied.

Slowly, he lowered her to her feet. "You look beautiful.

And you smell fantastic, too." The sweet scent sent blood rushing to his head and loins.

"Thank you," she said, still watching him closely.

They stood there, eyes locked, for what felt like forever, and at the same time it wasn't long enough.

"How have you been?" he asked in an attempt to break the silence. He didn't know about her, but his heart was pounding heavily in his chest.

Kelly stepped back, her eyes crinkling in a friendly smile. "I've been good. What about you?"

He looked at her. "Better now that you're here." Diamere reached out and captured her hand in his. "I guess I'd better introduce you to the crowd." What he really wanted to do was find a private spot where he could ravish her without several dozen eyes watching.

Her gaze traveled around the banquet room, taking in the residents laughing and eating, and her lips curled downward. "It doesn't look like this crowd needs volunteers."

"Actually, it was an excuse to get you here." As soon as her eyes widened, he held up his hands in surrender. "Seriously, I usually help make sure everyone is having a good time. I thought a beautiful woman would be a nice touch to help get these old hearts pumping."

Her face crinkled with laughter. "Okay, you're forgiven."

"Good." He took her hand again. "Let me introduce you to everyone, then."

They were all welcoming and eager to meet the girl on his arm. And Diamere was happier than he would have ever imagined to let the crowd know they were together. He introduced her to Mr. Brown, whose hand lingered on Kelly's waist a little too long. The women all commented on how pretty she was.

"Chile, I remember I used to have legs like that. I had men falling all over themselves," Ms. Childress said, and stuck out a meaty thigh with tan knee-highs that threatened to slip down to her ankles. Two other female residents crowded around Kelly, sharing beauty tips. Clearly amused when she raised her eyebrow in a signal for help, Diamere politely pulled her away and went in search of his grandmother.

Pressing close to his side, Kelly smiled up at him, eyes dancing with laughter. "Are they always like that?"

"Worse. Last year they invited a male stripper to Ms. Childress's ninetieth birthday bash."

Her eyes widened and they shared a laugh. The sound made his heart sing.

"Let me introduce you to Nana." He took Kelly's hand and felt a rush as she followed him over to the petite lady coming off the dance floor. As soon as she spotted them moving her way, Nana's face lit up.

"Well, who is this lovely thing?"

"Nana, this is my friend Kelly."

Extending her arms, Nana hugged her tightly. "Kelly. What a beautiful girl. I am so glad to finally meet you. My grandson has told me so much about you."

I did? Instead of saying anything, he just played along.

Kelly returned the embrace. "I've heard a lot about you, too," she said as she released her. The two began to talk, and soon Nana somehow managed to steer the conversation in a personal direction.

"Kelly, are you planning to get married and have babies anytime in the near future?"

She gave a nervous laugh. "Actually, I am someday, when the time is right."

Nana turned to Diamere. "You hear that? The woman wants a family."

He groaned. Nana didn't believe in beating around the bush.

Etta James's "At Last" came blazing from the juke-box. Diamere turned to Kelly and met her beautiful eyes. "Ms. Saunders, would you give me the honor of this dance?" he said, crooking his arm. The sooner he got her away from his grandmother the better.

"I would love to." Kelly latched onto his elbow and he led her through the crowd of residents already dancing slowly to the music. As soon as he found a clear spot, he pulled her close and locked his arms around her. Her wonderful scent filled his nose and he took a deep breath. It felt so right holding her.

All week, he had anxiously been awaiting the moment Kelly walked through that door. Now she was here, in his arms, and he didn't want to let her go. Why was that? What made her so different? He knew deep in his heart he wasn't yet ready to know the answer. All he knew for certain was that he wanted her in his life. He just needed to find a way to get her to realize she wanted him, as well. What he felt for her was too strong to ignore, too powerful to let go.

"Diamere?"

Her voice brought him back from his thoughts. He opened his eyes and looked down at the grin on her face.

"Yeah?"

"I think we can stop dancing. The song's been over for a while now."

His eyes traveled around the dance floor. Sure enough, the music had stopped and no one was on the floor but the two of them. Off to the side the residents of Shady Acres were watching and smiling knowingly.

With a silly grin, he reached inside his pocket for some change. "Let me go and put some more quarters in the box." He hurried over to the corner, selected a few songs and turned around in time to find Kelly dragging Mr. Brown onto the dance floor. Diamere crossed his arms over his chest and leaned against the jukebox, watching with amusement as the two moved to the Temptations. Kelly was definitely a hit.

"Care to dance, young man?"

He looked down at Ms. Pittman. The short, salt-and-pepper-haired widow had been responsible for tailoring many of his dress slacks. "I would love to." He took her arm and moved out onto the floor, following her lead.

The rest of the afternoon, he and Kelly took turns dancing with the residents, and he barely had a chance to get a few words in before someone else was pulling one of them onto the dance floor.

The sun had already started to set when the first group began heading back to their rooms. Diamere said his farewells and searched the crowd for Kelly, spotting her in the corner talking to Ms. Pittman and Nana. He moved over to the group and took his place beside her.

Kelly looked up at him and met his smile. "Hey. Nana and I were sharing coconut cake recipes."

Ms. Pittman dropped a hand to her thick waist. "Diamere, you better hurry up and marry her. This little lady here can cook."

Diamere looked down at his grandmother, whose eyes

softened as she watched him place his hand on Kelly's shoulder. He knew her well enough to know the wheels in her head were already turning.

Nana's smile mirrored approval. "A cook and a schoolteacher. I hope this isn't the last time I see you." She pointed a finger at Kelly. "Don't be a stranger."

"I won't, I promise." Leaning forward, Kelly kissed the elderly woman's cheek.

Diamere also kissed his grandmother. "Nana, I'm going to walk Kelly to her car."

"Take your time," she replied with a dismissive wave.

Hand in hand, Diamere walked Kelly to the door, waving to the others as they moved out to her Saturn in front of the retirement home. Once there, he curved his hands around her waist. "Thank you for coming."

"Thank you for inviting me." He noted her voice was a little shaky.

Diamere pulled her closer and she wrapped her arms around his neck. "When will I see you again?" he whispered against her cheek.

"Maybe before I leave for my grandparents' cottage."

"I hope so." He kissed her, keeping his touch gentle, giving her time to remember his taste, his smell. He used the tip of his tongue to ease her lips apart, then explored the fleshy softness of the inside of her mouth. When she gasped, he plunged deeper. Her body trembled and he desperately wanted everything she had to offer. Kelly slid her arms around his waist. Diamere briefly pulled back and stared down at her, then kissed her temple, her forehead, and down along her face to her neck before returning to her mouth again, where he savored the fruity taste of punch. Finally he broke off, breathing heavily. "I'll meet you at your house in an hour."

It wasn't a question or a request. It was a demand. Kelly met his eyes, then nodded. "Okay."

Chapter 14

It was almost nine when Kelly stepped inside her condo, heart still beating wildly against her chest. The evening had not gone at all as she had planned.

She moved to her room and reached for the zipper of her skirt and allowed the garment to fall in a heap on the floor, along with her blouse. Diamere was on his way, whether she liked it or not. Knowing that caused her pulse to race.

The past two weeks she'd done everything she could to forget about him and the passionate night they'd shared. But no matter how much she tried she could not rid herself of the memories. She lay awake aching to be with him, wishing things could have been different for both of them. She loved him; there was no denying that. But she knew her feelings were useless. From the beginning Diamere had made it clear he wasn't looking for anything serious. And her heart was too involved for just casual dating. All she would be doing was setting herself up for further heartache.

With a sigh, she finished undressing and moved over to her closet, removing a jungle-print caftan her sister had bought her while vacationing in the Bahamas last year. She slipped the soft cotton material over her head and smoothed it down her petite body. After sliding her feet inside her slippers, she went into the bathroom and gazed at her reflection in the mirror over the sink. Kelly gasped at what she saw. Her lips were swollen and her cheeks raw from Diamere's stubble. She looked like a woman who had been thoroughly kissed. What in the world was she doing, agreeing to see him again?

Dropping her eyes to the sink, Kelly knew the answer. Because she had to see him. The second she had walked into the building and spotted him standing across the banquet hall, her entire body had started trembling with need. And as soon as she was in his arms, dancing, she'd felt complete. She knew his touch, his smell, were the reasons her body, her soul, desperately needed to be near him.

Kelly splashed water on her face and reached for a towel just as she heard the doorbell chime. Her heartbeat accelerated. It was Diamere. Taking a deep breath, she let out the air slowly as she walked toward the door. She reached for the doorknob and paused, hand shaking. Once she allowed him to step across the threshold, there was no turning back.

She hesitated for a moment more. *You can do this. You can do this.* Finally, she turned the knob and opened it.

Kelly could barely catch her breath at the sight of Diamere standing there under the dim porch light. For a second she stood perfectly still, just looking at him and thinking about how much she loved him.

Diamere moved toward her and before she realized what was happening, he'd pushed the door closed and was pressing his body to hers and kissing her. His lips sought entrance to her mouth and as his tongue dipped inside, a moan escaped her lips. She was startled at the feel of his arousal pulsing hard against her stomach. His hands slid along the curve of her back and settled on her bottom. The heat of his hands burned through her clothes.

Even though she knew being in his arms was a mistake, she arched her body against his, responding in every feminine way possible. Seemingly of their own accord, she soon found her arms wrapped around his neck.

Diamere groaned, tangling their tongues in an urgent rhythm that both frightened and inflamed her. She could never grow tired of kissing him. Oh, how she loved the way he tasted. Sweet and masculine. Warm, wet and passionate. She was on fire and completely aroused, and a deep yearning throbbed below. She knew that she loved this man and had willingly given him her body, which now hummed with need for him to join the two of them as one. She also knew she truly had to end things before they got way out of hand. But before she ended their relationship once and for all, she wanted Diamere to make love to her one more time.

Diamere stared down at her and for the longest time the only sound was their breathing. Kelly gazed back at him, breathless with anticipation, waiting to see what he said or did next.

Finally, after what felt like forever, Diamere cupped

her face with his hands. "When I saw you walk into Shady Acres today, I forgot everything. All I wanted to do was touch you and hold you, and especially kiss you. Once we danced I knew there was no way I could go one more day without being inside of you."

All Kelly could do was nod as his hand moved to the curve of her neck, gently stroking her. Barely contained desire traveled between them, too powerful for either of them to ignore.

"Yes, I want you, too," she murmured, and her core flared in response to the desire and overwhelming need they both had acknowledged.

Diamere rested both hands on her hips and pulled her closer. Desire blazed in his eyes. He bent his head to kiss her, brushing her lips with his in that oh-so-seductive way he had. She responded, returning the kiss, her body leaning into his.

Moving, Diamere rested his mouth on her neck, sending a wave of heat over her sensitive skin. "I could kiss you all night," he whispered as he pulled away, "but I want to taste the rest of you, as well."

She moaned aloud, reacting to his seductive voice. She wanted him badly, and she wanted him now.

Diamere steered her back against the wall, stroking his hands over her buttocks and thighs possessively. He ended their kiss and Kelly practically cried in protest.

"Which way is your room?" he asked.

She tried to steady her nerves but her heart thudded out a violent rhythm and her body buzzed with anticipation. "That way." She pointed a shaky finger toward the end of the hall.

Diamere lifted her effortlessly into his arms, carried her down the hallway and into the first bedroom on the right, where he set her on her feet. Slowly, he raised her caftan up around her thighs, caressing her with his hands. "I've wanted to see you naked all night, from the moment you stepped into that room." Kelly willingly held her arms in the air and allowed him to slide it over her head.

"You're more beautiful than I remember," he whispered as he stared at her bare breasts appreciatively. He slid a teasing finger along the top of her lace panties, making her shiver with need, then slid them down to her ankles, bending to kiss her stomach in the process. She swayed, clutching his shoulders, overwhelmed with burning desire. Again, he lifted her into his arms and carried her to the bed. Diamere lay beside her, his hands stroking her stomach, traveling to her inner thighs, then easing her legs apart, his mouth moving toward the source of her heat.

"Diamere!" she cried, before she felt his tongue at the juncture there. Never would she have imagined that this would feel so good. He licked and nibbled and explored her body. His tongue traveled deep, causing her to lift her hips off the bed.

"Diamere," she murmured again, her head falling back against the pillows. She moaned and twisted on the bed while his tongue took possession of her most sensitive area. Pleasure roared through her body. Her release hit her, fast and deep, but Diamere didn't let up, and the combination of his hands and his mouth on her was too much.

"Please!" she begged. She was desperate for him to finish what he had started. She wanted it all—to feel the touch of his bare skin on hers and the thrust of his body inside her.

Diamere stood up, eyeing her possessively as he took off his shirt and tossed it on the floor. He kicked off his shoes and undid his slacks. She admired the dark hair on his chest, tapering into a distinct line that led her eyes down to his groin. She watched with a growing desire as he removed his pants, followed by his boxers. Diamere was long and beautifully thick. He reached for his wallet from his pants pocket and pulled out a condom, ripping it open, then rolling it onto his length. When he climbed over her, she reveled in the sensation of his warm, muscular body between her legs. She was ready for him. Within seconds, he began to ease inside her and she moaned. He swore under his breath when he felt her inner muscles tighten around him, and drove his full length inside of her. Each thrust was full and she felt complete. A sob built at the back of her throat. She locked her legs around him as she met his strokes.

"I need this," Diamere whispered close to her ear. "I need to be inside of you."

And so do I, she thought, just as she cried out from pleasure. He deepened his strokes, drawing them both closer to the edge. Rising up on his arms, he pressed his mouth to hers and slipped his tongue inside. Kelly was powerless to do anything but enjoy. She was in complete ecstasy. The rhythm of their lovemaking spread the heat of imminent climax through her body. Their tempo increased and each stroke was accompanied by orgasmic groans of pleasure. Kelly rocked her hips, meeting his thrusts with her own until she cried out with release.

"Oh yes…yes," Diamere urged, his eyes blazing with passion. She felt his whole body arch against hers and he climaxed with a mighty roar.

Moments later, while she was still gasping and clutching at his shoulders in the aftermath of their lovemaking, he reached down and began stroking her from shoulder to hip.

"We're not done yet," he whispered, and he lowered his mouth back down to hers, melting her into submission all over again.

Diamere rolled out of bed, needing to put some distance between himself and Kelly. He walked down the hall to her kitchen and retrieved a bottle of water from the fridge, then went to the sliding glass door, opened it and stepped onto the deck for some fresh air. Being with Kelly again awakened a desire too powerful to ignore.

The evening wasn't supposed to be more than the retirement center dance. He'd thought her presence would be enough, that all he needed was to see and talk to her. Instead, after holding her in his arms, all he could think about was making love to her. Okay, so maybe he wasn't being completely honest. Maybe he had wished, had hoped, that the night would end with her lying naked in his bed. But he hadn't been a hundred percent certain it would happen.

Once it had, it was just as explosive as before.

Diamere leaned against the railing of the deck and stared up at the dark, starlit sky. Why now? Why were things with Kelly so different? Instead of running away, he couldn't wait to go back to the bedroom and hold her in his arms. He loved waking up feeling her soft, warm skin. Even now the erotic image of her slid across his mind, taunting him.

Unable to stay away from her a second longer, he

finished the bottle of water and made his way back down the hall. But instead of entering the room, he stood by the door and watched Kelly, fighting the hard thumping of his heart.

In her sleep she arched and stretched, and he held his breath and watched as she kicked the coverlet away. She was an erotic dream. The sheets tangled around her slender waist, revealing the dip of her navel and leaving her full, heavy breasts exposed. A slim arm was flung across a satin pillow, while one slender leg had slipped from beneath the sheets.

Diamere felt heat flow to his loins. He stepped into the room and climbed back under the covers. He felt like pinching himself to make certain what just happened really had. But he was here, feeling worn-out and completely satisfied. Never, not even with Ryan, had a woman made him feel the way he'd just felt with Kelly. Not that he was complaining. Good sex was hard to find. But that still didn't stop him from wondering if someone had just hit him over the head, because he had no idea what was happening to him. Instead of thinking up a reason to leave, he wanted to find any excuse to stay in her bed until Monday.

Diamere took a deep breath as realization sank in. He should have known it was going to be special between them. He had always felt in his heart that they would be good together. Now he had proof. *What am I going to do?*

"What are you thinking about?" Kelly's voice sliced through his thoughts.

He shifted on the bed and gazed down at her, lying curled up beside him. "I'm thinking about you."

From beneath her eyelashes she gazed up at him. "What about me?"

"Making love to you again."

She pursed her lips and made a sound that sounded like a purr. "Really?" She giggled. "Let's see just how badly you really want me." She pushed the sheet away and stared down at his crotch. Diamere felt the heat of her gaze as he pulsed against her thigh.

"Wow! I guess you do want me." She laughed unsteadily and sat up, tossing the wild fall of her hair away from her eyes. Kelly wrapped her hand around the base of his hard length and ran her thumb across the tip. Diamere sucked in a shaky breath. Her lack of experience, coupled with her curiosity and willingness to learn, was enough to drive him insane with desire.

"You're growing right beneath my fingers," she said as she looked at him and he pulsed a second time.

Diamere trailed his hand up her ribs to her breasts. Instantly, her nipples sprang to life and her lips parted. "It means that I want you, again," Diamere said seductively.

She released him and tilted her head so that she could meet his eyes, and smiled. The moonlight illuminated her face. Diamere ran his thumb across her lips. Then he gently flipped her onto her back and pinned her hands to her sides. "Tell me. What do you want?"

She stared up at him and he brought his lips down onto hers. His mouth traveled to her neck and he noticed the sharp intake of her breath. "I'm still waiting," he reminded her.

"I want you," she moaned.

"Look at me." When Kelly stared up at him, he said, "Now tell me again."

"I want you, Diamere."

For the rest of the night he would focus on making love to her. He would worry about the consequences later.

Chapter 15

The alarm went off at six o'clock on Monday. Kelly hit the snooze button and continued to lie there. Her eyelids were heavy and she felt as if she had just fallen asleep. In fact, she had. She'd had less than four hours sleep.

And it was all Diamere's fault.

Last night she had slipped under the covers with him heavy on the brain. Warm milk hadn't helped. And reading proved to be a big waste of time because she read the same paragraph three times and didn't comprehend a single line. Ever since Diamere had come into her life she'd been feeling slightly off balance. Her days were no longer her own. He had invaded her mind and taken over her thoughts and actions. All she could do was think about him.

Kelly kept playing Saturday night over and over again in her head. His kisses. His taste. Him lying between her legs making love to her. *Enough!* All she was doing was torturing herself.

She had been avoiding him since they had last seen each other. She had even taken the rest of the week off to enjoy some time to herself before she left for the lake, but now she was going crazy because she didn't have enough to occupy her time. Even trying to work on her thesis was a big waste of time because she just couldn't focus.

The phone rang, interrupting her thoughts. Kelly reached over for the cordless phone and brought it to her ear.

"Wake up, sleepyhead."

Her lips curled upward at the sound of her big sister's voice. "What are you doing up this early?" Calaine was in Missouri, and since it was six in Delaware, it was five in the Midwest.

"I had to pee. And I knew you would be up."

Kelly rolled onto her side. "Yep, like clockwork. How are David and the kids?"

"Wonderful."

There was something her sister wasn't telling her. "What? There's something on your mind. I can hear it in your voice."

Calaine hesitated for a moment. "Look, you know you can tell me anything," Kelly assured her.

"Kelly, I'm pregnant."

She sprang up in the bed. "Oh my goodness! That is wonderful! When is the baby due?"

"In January. And I'm so hoping for another girl. You know David wants a boy." Calaine's voice rang with happiness.

"Of course."

"Don't tell Mama. I want to surprise her when we come down for Thanksgiving."

"My lips are sealed." Kelly cradled the phone against her shoulder as she reached for her robe at the end of the bed and slipped her arms through it. "Oh my gosh, congratulations."

"Thanks. So tell me, what's been going on with you? Found a new man yet?"

Kelly giggled. Leave it to her big sister to get straight to the point. "Something like that. An old relationship renewed. Do you remember the best man at Mark and Essence's wedding?"

"The fine one with the deep dimples?"

Kelly exhaled. Damn, she loved his dimples. "Yep, that's the one."

"Ooh! I want to hear all about this."

"I figured you would." Kelly moved into the kitchen, and as she prepared her coffee, she told Calaine everything there was to tell about Diamere Redmond.

"I can hear in your voice that he's special to you," Calaine commented at the end of Kelly's early-morning confession.

"He is. I just…" She struggled with her words. "I just don't know if a relationship is meant for us. I mean, both of us made it clear we weren't looking for anything. But now that we…made love, I realize there is no way I can separate my body from my heart. I want more than he is willing to give me. But on the other hand, I'm afraid to take that chance again."

"Again? Devin was a jerk. He doesn't count. I didn't like him from the second I met him."

Calaine had been in Texas at a human resources convention when Kelly drove down to Austin with

Devin so they could meet. The three of them went to dinner. She'd hated to admit it, but the evening had been a disaster. Devin complained about the meal and the service and chastised the waitress until she was in tears.

"Why didn't you tell me?" Kelly asked now.

"Because you were in love and I didn't want to do anything to jeopardize your happiness."

She sighed into the receiver. "Yeah, well, you see where your silence got me."

"Next time I'll come out with it, trust me. I can say that I liked Diamere the second Mark introduced him to me."

Kelly couldn't help but smile. "He's a wonderful person."

"And you're in love with him."

Kelly lowered herself onto a seat at the kitchen table. "Is it that obvious?"

"Yep. And if I can tell over the phone, I can just imagine what your eyes are saying."

Her mother always said she could tell what Kelly was thinking just by looking her in the eye. The last thing she needed was for Diamere to know what she was feeling, which was why she couldn't wait until tomorrow to head down to the lake. She needed that time to think and get her head straight before school started in a week. "No matter how I feel, I'm not looking for anything serious, and neither is he."

"How do you know his feelings haven't changed? Have you asked him?"

"Hell no."

"Then you can only speak for yourself."

Kelly hated when Calaine was right. "I am really not ready for that."

"Okay. I'm not going to push you but I think you should give it some thought. I'd hate to see you lose something that only comes around once in a lifetime."

They chatted a little longer about the kids and their upcoming visit, then Kelly said goodbye and disconnected the call.

She prepared herself a cup of coffee and stepped out back to take a seat in her wicker patio chair, resting her feet on the matching ottoman. While she sipped her coffee, Kelly thought about her conversation with her sister. Just thinking about Diamere caused her body to tingle. Closing her eyes, she could vividly picture his face. She inhaled and thought she caught a whiff of his natural scent. What was wrong with her? She hadn't felt anything like this with Devin.

Because you didn't really love him.

She definitely hadn't experienced any of these feelings with Devin. Never did her palms sweat just at the mention of his name. Her heart had never felt as if it were going to explode from her chest each and every time she was in his presence. Those were things she only felt with Diamere.

She finished her coffee and stepped back into the house, deciding she needed to do something other than think about Diamere all day. Since the weatherman had forecast another scorching August afternoon, she spent the rest of the morning straightening up the house and after lunch she organized her picture albums, a project she'd been planning to get to all summer long.

She was on her way back into her bedroom when she heard her cell phone ring. Kelly picked it up and noticed she had a new text message from a number she didn't recognize.

Come to Hadley's 2nite at 10. Luv 2 C U.

Her heart pounded heavily with excitement. Diamere wanted to see her tonight. She contemplated the idea for a moment, then talked herself out of going. The best thing to do was to keep her distance. She was already in way over her head. She was leaving for the cottage in the morning, and the sooner the better. It was a ninety-mile drive and the farther she was away from him, the better off she would be.

Chapter 16

Diamere moved to the VIP section of Hadley, to a large round table where his cousins the Beaumonts—Jabarie, Jace, Jaden, Bianca, and their spouses—were sitting, just as a second bottle of Moët champagne was being delivered.

"When I said drinks were on the house I didn't mean put me out of business," Diamere declared with laughter in his voice.

"You can afford it."

He met the smile of Jace, the oldest of the group, as he reached for the bottle. "You forget, my last name isn't Beaumont."

"True, but tonight it seems the hottest name in this joint is my cousin, Diamere Redmond."

Jaden rose from his seat, locks hanging loose around his broad shoulders. "I want to make a toast." He waited until everyone around the table had raised their glasses. "To Diamere. May he have many years of success."

"Hear. Hear."

They all clinked glasses and took a sip from their flutes.

"Thanks, everyone," Diamere replied, grinning. Then he glanced off to his left for the umpteenth time.

"What's up, man? Are you expecting Publishers Clearance House?"

"What?" Diamere replied, realizing Jaden was talking to him. "Why do you say that?"

Jaden grinned knowingly. "Because you've been watching the door all night."

Jabarie nodded. "He's right."

"It's gotta be a girl," Bianca said between sips.

Jace frowned at that idea. "I doubt a woman could have that much of his attention. After Ryan, the last thing Diamere wants is another woman."

Sheyna nudged her husband in the shoulder. "Are you saying I never had your attention like that?"

London tossed his hands in the air. "Man, if I was you, I'd be very careful how I answered that question."

The whole group laughed.

"See, I got this one trained well," Bianca said, and dropped a kiss on London's cheek. A look of adoration appeared in her husband's eyes.

Diamere shook his head, smiling at the new king of Clarence's Infamous Chicken and Fish House. Selling his family restaurant to the couple was the smartest business move he'd ever made, besides purchasing the clubs. London and Bianca Beaumont Brown had barely been married eighteen months and were already the proud parents of a baby girl.

Diamere checked his watch. It was after ten. If Kelly didn't arrive in the next ten minutes, he would give up looking for her.

When Jace had called him that afternoon and told him the couples were planning to come to Philly for a night on the town, he'd felt the overwhelming urge to have Kelly with him. He didn't know why, but he wanted her to meet his family.

Jabarie hopped from his chair and grabbed his wife's hand. "Come on, Brenna baby. Let's show these old folks how to two-step." She rose slowly because of the protruding stomach. The couple was expecting their fifth child in the spring.

Jace gave a rude snort. "That's why they have all them babies. He can't keep his hands off his wife."

Drawing the small beauty into his arms, Jabarie nuzzled Brenna's cheek lovingly, then fixed his gaze on his older brother. "Don't hate because my wife loves her man."

Chuckling, Jace rose. "Bro, you know you can't dance." There was a hint of challenge in his voice. For as long as Diamere had been around his cousins, the oldest two had always found something to compete about.

Jabarie glanced around the table. "Y'all are our witnesses."

Jaden, the youngest brother, rose and held out his hand to his wife, Danica, a former runway model. "Come on, sweetie. Let's show them how it's done."

She tossed her long auburn hair away from her face, then accepted the proffered hand. "Jaden, dear, promise you won't step on my feet."

Bianca tipped her head back, laughing. "Some things never change, do they, big brother?"

"Ha-ha. Very funny." He draped his arm around Danica's waist and escorted her onto the crowded dance floor.

Diamere lowered himself into a seat at the head of the table and watched the couples dance. Danica was right. Jaden still had two left feet. But Jace and Sheyna definitely knew how to move. So did Jabarie and Brenna. Out the corner of his eye, he saw that Bianca and London were too busy gazing at each other to notice who was the better dancer. Diamere kicked his baby cousin's foot under the table. "Bianca, you need to pay attention."

She rolled her eyes as she looked across the table. "You need to mind your own business," she said without malice. "It isn't often that London and I get a little time by ourselves without Sierra." Their daughter had just turned thirteen months old.

The song ended and the music slowed. More couples moved onto the dance floor. Bianca dragged her husband out, and Diamere, slowly stroking his chin, watched all four couples move to the beat of the music. London was holding Bianca as if she meant the world to him. *This was love.*

He couldn't help but think about Kelly. If only things had been different there was no telling what might have happened between them. Or still could if he allowed it.

He shook off the thought because there was no way he was setting himself up for failure again. He just couldn't. The last time had hurt so bad he never wanted to endure that kind of pain again. Yet a part of him yearned for what his cousins had all found. Stability. Family. And most importantly, love.

The hairs on the back of his neck stood up just then

and Diamere glanced over his shoulder. His heart thumped in his chest when he spotted Kelly hovering near the entrance. Instantly, he rose from his seat and closed the distance between them. The nearer he got the faster his heart beat. He knew the exact moment she recognized him. Her lips curled upward and her eyes sparkled with mischief.

Diamere took a moment to peruse her figure in that short, glimmering, pink sequined dress with thin straps. On her feet were fuchsia heels that made her legs appear as long and lean as they ever did. As soon as he reached her, he dipped his head and captured her mouth in a long, searing kiss, publicly declaring for anyone to see that she was there for him.

When he pulled back and straightened, Kelly struggled with her words. "I guess that means you're happy to see me."

A smile crinkled Diamere's eyes and his magnificent mouth. "Yes, I didn't think you would come."

"I wasn't going to," she heard herself admit, "but I decided it was better than spending an evening curled up in bed watching old movies."

"There's nothing wrong with lying in bed watching movies when you have someone else curled up beside you."

Kelly gazed up into his eyes, her heart pounding a heavy rhythm in sync with the music thumping from the nearby speaker. She still didn't understand why she had come. She knew every reason for why keeping her distance was the way to go, especially after the other night. She had been so caught up in the moment when he made love to her that the words *I love you* had practically escaped from her lips. Yet, as she looked up and saw the desire burning in the depths of his eyes, she knew nothing could have stopped her from being here tonight. And seeing him move across the floor dressed in dark chocolate slacks and a silk cream shirt, with a single diamond stud in his left ear, Kelly knew she had made the right decision.

Accepting his proffered hand, she followed Diamere to a large round table where several other couples were sitting. As soon as they spotted the two of them, she was met by several curious stares. Diamere stopped and draped his arm across her shoulders, then smiled down at her as if to make sure everything was okay. Kelly nodded.

He turned to the group. "Everyone, I would like you to meet Kellis Saunders."

His introduction was followed by a series of warm welcomes. Kelly glanced around the table at the four couples and smiled. It seemed all eyes were on her.

A tall man with a smooth pecan complexion and shoulder-length locks rose and offered her his hand. "It's a pleasure to meet you, Kellis."

"Please, call me Kelly," she replied, nervously clearing her throat.

Diamere pointed to the couple on the end. "Kelly, this is my cousin Jaden and his wife, Danica."

Kelly gazed at the beautiful woman in surprise. "You look so familiar."

"I used to model," Danica said with a shrug.

She blinked as recognition hit. "I've seen you in *Ebony* magazine."

Jaden gazed at his wife adoringly. "She used to be

the finest thang on the runway. Still is as far as I'm concerned."

Danica covered his mouth with her hand. "Jaden, you're embarrassing me."

Smiling, he dipped his head and pressed his lips to hers. Kelly didn't miss the looks they gave each other. As she watched the couple interact, it was clear the two were so in love they practically glowed.

A woman stepped up beside her, and Kelly found her smile genuine and warm. "Forgive my cousins. I'm Bianca Beaumont Brown and that there is my husband, London." She pointed to the tall dark man sitting at the end of the table, waving at her.

"Oh my God! I remember seeing the two of you in the society section last year." Kelly's eyes traveled over to London. "You own Clarence's Infamous Chicken and Fish House."

Diamere laughed. "Yep. That's the chicken king."

Nodding, London reached for the glass in front of him. "That's me."

Kelly remembered reading about London taking over the reins not long ago.

Diamere pulled her closer, his hand moving gently down her back. "Over there are my cousins Jabarie and Jace, and their wives, Brenna and Sheyna."

A smile tipped the corners of Sheyna's lips. "Girlfriend, you are wearing the hell out of that dress!"

"Yes, you are," Diamere murmured close to her ear, and she met his gaze again.

Brenna smiled and rubbed her stomach, as if she felt the baby kick. "Sheyna and I will have to take you with us on our shopping trip next month. Maybe you can give us some fashion tips."

"Absolutely, although you both look fabulous," Kelly replied, flattered they'd include her in their plans.

Jace looked over at Sheyna and groaned. "Watch out, Kelly. These women are serious shoppers."

The music changed to Jaheim. Diamere gave Kelly a gentle tug. "Excuse me, but I need to hold this little lady in my arms."

Kelly followed his lead out onto the dance floor just as the slow song began. Glancing over her shoulder, she checked to see if the others were following, but they just sat there staring and grinning.

"I think your family is watching us," she murmured as Diamere pulled her into his arms.

He glanced over at the table in turn and then down at her. "Then let's give them a show." Before she had a chance to find out what he meant, he lowered his head and kissed her in the middle of the dance floor, in front of his family and anyone else who bothered to look their way.

When he finally pulled away, Kelly tilted her head back and stared up into his eyes, shocked at how open Diamere was with his affection.

"What changed your mind about coming out tonight?"

"You," she said. "I wanted to see you."

A grin tipped the corner of Diamere's lips. "Well, I'm glad you came."

"So am I."

He lowered his head and kissed her again. When he pulled back, her own head was spinning. The man sure knew how to lay it on her.

They finished up the dance and returned to the table. Over the next few hours his family made sure she felt right at home. Diamere sat beside her with his hand on her knee, causing her blood to race.

It was shortly after midnight when Bianca rose from her chair. "Thanks for a wonderful evening, but Sierra should be wide-awake by now and ready for her late-night feeding."

Kelly didn't miss the motherly pride in her voice.

Jabarie rose. "Yeah, we probably need to be heading back to Sheraton Beach ourselves." The others rose, as well. Diamere and Kelly bade them goodbye.

"All of you have a safe trip home," Diamere said. They were moving across the floor when Kelly finished the last of her drink and got up from her seat. Diamere's brow rose. "You're leaving, too?"

She nodded. "Yep. I want to get an early start in the morning."

He took her hand and pulled her close to him. "Come home with me."

Kelly wanted to but knew it would be a mistake. Her body already yearned for what only he could give her. "I don't think that's a good idea tonight, but I'll give you a call when I get back from the lake."

He didn't push. Instead he nodded. "I'd like that. Let me walk you to your car." He placed a hand on the small of her back and escorted her through the club and out across the parking lot.

Tilting her head slightly, she looked up at him, and there it was between them again—passion, desire, love. Once more the emotions rendered her helpless, unable to move or combat what she was feeling.

Diamere must have felt it, too, because his breathing had changed. "Kelly," he muttered softly.

"Yes," she replied, her voice barely audible.

He pushed her back against her car and began kissing her. His mouth was delicious, urgent and demanding of a response she was more than willing to give. The intensity between them was mind-boggling. No matter how much she tried to pretend she didn't love him, her feelings had intensified. Her desire for him was relentless. Diamere's hands searched her body, touching every trembling part of her as his mouth crushed hers. Unable to control what she was feeling, Kelly started an exploration of her own, sliding her palms beneath his shirt and along the powerful muscles of his back and chest. Murmuring her name against her mouth, he ran his hands across her breasts, stopping long enough to allow his thumbs to graze her nipples. Desire made her senses spin as she cried out and arched her spine, bringing her breasts closer to his touch. A feverous fire raged through her. The confines of her clothing frustrated her. She wanted him to touch her bare skin.

Slowly, Diamere raised his head. He made no attempt to move. Instead he stared down at her, his eyes glazed with passion.

"Follow me home. I want to make love to you." His voice was as thick as if he had been running. She knew exactly how he felt, because her own heart was still racing.

"I can't," she began, and was cut off as his mouth closed over hers again, forcing her lips apart. Tongues intertwined while his hands slid down the curve of her hips, thrusting her against him so that she could feel the evidence of his arousal.

"You know what you do to me," he muttered.

"Yes, I feel it." She tightened her arms around his

neck and curved herself closer. She loved the way she felt, being in his arms with his weight against her.

A car door slamming brought her back to her senses. Gasping, she turned her head and pushed at him gently. "Look, I've got to go."

Diamere grabbed her arm to keep her from leaving. "Why are you running away from us?"

Breathing heavily, she kept her eyes averted from his masculine presence. "Because I've been down this path before and am not the least bit interested in traveling that route again."

Diamere placed a hand to her chin and tilted her face so she had no choice but to look at him as he spoke. "You can't base our relationship on your past experiences. That's unfair."

She saw the look of hurt on his face and wanted so desperately to leap into his arms. Instead she stepped back, putting a little distance between them. "Life isn't fair. Unfortunately, I have other things going on in my life right now that have to take priority."

"So what now?"

She could tell he put his pride on the line in asking that question. Kelly shook her head and decided to be honest. "I don't know."

He reached out for her but she stepped back before he could touch her. If she felt the heat of his skin against hers, there was no way she would be able to resist him a second longer.

"I'll call you," she said, then climbed in her car and pulled away without looking back.

Chapter 17

Diamere leaned forward in the chair behind his desk. From the way Carlos was having a hard time standing up on his own, he knew it would be one of those nights.

"Carlos, what can I do for you?"

The man crossed his arms and had the nerve to glare at him and say, "I want my job back."

Diamere stood to his full height, feeling every bit of his thirty-five years as he came from behind the desk to stare at the man he'd once considered a friend. "I can't do that."

"Why?"

He met his intense glare head-on. "Because you're an alcoholic, and unless you're willing to get help, the answer is no."

Carlos swayed to the side, lost his footing and stumbled. "I can't pay my rent."

Diamere stared down at the sad man. "I'll tell you

what," he began. "You check yourself into rehab and I'll take care of your bills for you."

Carlos gave him a look of skepticism. "You would do that for me?"

He had to take a step back. Carlos's breath reeked of alcohol. "Yes, that's what friends do."

His ex-employee paused, then nodded his head. "Okay. I'll do it."

"Good. Go get some rest. Tony, I need you to take him home."

The large club manager shifted his weight and nodded. "Sure thing, boss."

Diamere watched them leave. He wouldn't wish that kind of ill fortune on anyone. Carlos once had had the world at this fingertips and a beautiful woman on his arm. Unfortunately, he'd let his popularity with the other ladies break up his engagement. He'd ended up losing his woman and later regretted his choices. Now he tried to hide behind alcohol.

Regret.

Crossing his arms against his chest, Diamere paced the length of his office. Regret was one thing he never wanted to feel. Yet he was already there. He regretted letting Kelly walk out of his club tonight. He regretted leaving her seven years ago. The last thing he wanted was to look back on his life and regret letting her walk out of his life for good.

Hours after arriving home, Kelly lay in bed still waiting for her heart to slow down. She loved Diamere. There was no thinking about it. She knew what she felt in her heart, and being with him tonight proved she couldn't keep going on like this. Something had to give. The question was what?

There was a knock at her door and it startled her. She rose from the bed and moved down the hall to the front door. "Who is it?"

"Kelly, it's me. Open the door."

Her heart started pounding. Hand shaking, she reached for the lock and opened it. As soon as she met the whites of Diamere's eyes, she took a deep breath and fought the instinct to jump into his arms. "Why are you here?" she asked as she searched his eyes for answers.

"You know why I'm here."

He covered the distance between them, pulled her into his arms and captured her lips. Her arms came around him as she gave in to everything she was feeling. She could regret her decision later.

Diamere brought his mouth to hers and for an instant she was simply too stunned to speak. His intentions were clear. Kelly could feel the hard evidence of his arousal pressed against her abdomen. She wanted to take it out, to feel it in her hand. He deepened the kiss and she tasted the virility that was all male. When his tongue slid between her lips, the fire between them sparked to life, and whatever he wanted was all that mattered.

Kelly slipped her arms around his neck and returned the kiss. His hands found her breasts and he began to caress them, cupping them through the soft nylon gown, teasing her nipples until they hardened. Unconsciously, she arched toward him, pressing the fullness of her breasts into his hands.

"You like this?" he asked.

"Yes," she moaned as a sliver of heat ran through her.

"Since you left the club, I couldn't stop thinking about you," he said. "I couldn't stay away a minute longer."

Diamere kissed her cheek, her neck, and found her lips again. She felt his hands sliding over her bottom, cupping her and pulling her against his hardness. He was clearly aroused, and so was she. No matter what happened tomorrow or the day after, she wanted this, wanted him.

He reached toward her, loosening the buttons on her gown, and eased the material off her shoulders and down over her hips, into a pool at her feet.

"Put your arms around my neck," he instructed, his fingers circling her waist, easing her toward him. Kelly followed his command and looked up at him, tall and handsome, his eyes so very dark, and there was something about being completely naked while he was still clothed that turned her on.

"You are so beautiful," he said. His gaze held hers as his hands caressed her bottom. "Open your legs."

Her body pulsed, tightened. The look in his eyes promised a pleasure she knew he was capable of giving her.

"Diamere, I—"

"Open your legs," he commanded.

Her heartbeat raced at the deep tone of authority. Heat settled between her thighs, and desire flowed through her blood. She did as he commanded, and felt his hands running over her bottom, slipping between her legs, and then he began to stroke her as he unbuckled his pants.

Shyness and eagerness overcame her. Diamere stopped caressing her long enough to reach inside his wallet for protection. When he put the condom in her hand, Kelly glanced up at him with uncertainty. She didn't have the slightest idea what to do, yet found herself ripping the package open and sliding the latex over his length.

"Wrap your legs around me."

Diamere lifted her off the floor of the living room. She twined her legs tightly around his body and used the cool wall as support. Immediately, she felt his hardened length probing for entrance. When he slid deep into her, she arched her back and closed her eyes.

Diamere gripped her hips, holding her in place to receive his deep thrusts. Her own need heightened and her body tightened around him. She sighed with pleasure as release shook her. Diamere pounded into her until he took his own release, a low groan slipping from his throat.

They spiraled down together, Diamere still standing with her pressed against the wall. He lowered his mouth and captured hers in a powerful kiss, then swept her up into his arms.

"I'm taking you to bed."

Her pulse raced as he carried her down the hall to her room and set her gently on the bed. While her eyes were on him, he removed his clothes, then slid his body on top of hers. The second time they made love was even more powerful, and after they both cried out in pleasure, they stayed there in each other's arms and drifted off to sleep.

Hours later, Kelly woke to find Diamere staring down at her, his eyes intense with thought.

"We need to talk," he said.

She turned her head and glanced over at the alarm clock on the nightstand. It was after seven. Had she really slept that late? She had expected to be on the highway by six in hopes of missing some of the beach traffic. But now a wave of desire swept through her, reminding her how comfortable she had felt with her body snuggled up against his. "What would you like to talk about?" she asked in a groggy voice.

"Us," Diamere replied, as if her question was ridiculous. It took her a second to realize the seriousness of his expression.

Wiping her eyes, Kelly sat up in bed. "Last I checked, there was no us."

"Yes, but things have changed."

Then tell me you love me. She yearned to hear those three words. "What has changed?"

Diamere dragged a frustrated hand across his face, then met her intense stare. "I'm not ready for our relationship to end."

Kelly pursed her lips with disappointment. It wasn't exactly what she wanted to hear, but at least it was a start. "Why is that?"

"Why do you think?" Diamere said as he looked up and down her naked body with a soft laugh.

Kelly gave a weak smile. Her shoulders sagged in response. All he wanted was for the sex to continue, without any commitment. Just like a man. "That's not good enough," she replied with a proud tilt of her chin.

"And why the hell not?" he barked.

Because I love you. Kelly swallowed the lump in her throat. "I already told you. Because I don't have time for a relationship right now. I've got too much going on in my life and it would be selfish of me."

"And what if I want to be selfish?"

Kelly snorted. "It doesn't matter what you want."

She swung the covers away, then rose from the bed and padded across the room for her robe, which was draped across a chaise in the corner. "This is not up for discussion." She slipped into the pink flannel garment and tied the belt before turning around.

Diamere gave a frustrated sigh, then rose from the bed, as well. He stood there in all his naked glory. He was hard and ready for action. The mere sight of him made Kelly feel dizzy with lust.

"I like having you in my life. What's so wrong with that?" he asked.

Everything. There was no way she could continue to be with him and not fall deeper in love with him. Her heart was on the line and it prevented her from thinking coherently.

"Listen, Diamere, I really enjoyed being with you, but it's time for me to get back to my life." She cleared her throat uncomfortably. "I guess I'd better get ready. I planned to leave for the lake hours ago. A few days out in the country is just what I need right now."

She waited, hoping he would say or do something. Instead he stood there for the longest time before he finally reached down for his clothes. "I don't know what to say to get you to change your mind."

Just tell me you love me. "Diamere, nothing will change my mind. We both made it clear that we weren't looking for anything serious. Nothing has changed. At least not for me. But school is starting in a week and I really need to get back on track or I'll never get my thesis done."

He slipped into his pants, then moved to where she was standing. It took everything she had not to wrap her arms around him and ask him to hold her.

"We could find a way to work around each other's schedules," Diamere suggested. "I like what you and I have."

She swallowed. If only he would tell her he loved her, she would feel more comfortable in making time for him in her life. "I'm sorry. I didn't expect things to be this…"

"Intense? This powerful?" Diamere asked. "Well, neither did I, but it's not going away. We have some sort of connection that has survived and ignited after all these years. And if anything, it just seems to get stronger each time I see you."

Kelly backed away, needing to put a little distance between them. She loved him so much and was hurting inside. "I know what you mean, but I just can't do this. I'm sorry, Diamere, but this relationship is over."

With nothing else to say, she went in search of her slippers. Her knees were wobbling as she moved down the hall and found them in the living room. Seconds later, Diamere followed. He moved to the door and paused. She held her breath, heart pounding, and waited. Diamere stood in place for so long she thought he was about to say something, before he finally reached for the door and opened it.

"Have a safe trip, okay?"

She nodded as she swallowed back a sob and watched him walk out of her life.

Chapter 18

"Diamere, your mind is definitely not with us."

Hearing his name, he whipped his head around to look up at the three J's—Jabarie, Jace and Jaden. All of them were staring at him.

"How are we going to bowl if you're a million miles away?" Shaking his shoulder-length locks, Jaden reached for his bowling ball and within seconds sent it flying down the lane.

Trying to push his thoughts aside, Diamere grabbed his beer and took a drink. "I've just got a lot on my mind."

"Anything you care to share?" Jabarie asked.

"Nope," he replied. It was his turn to bowl. He rose, picked up his ball and sent it flying in turn, knocking down every pin that was bold enough to stand in its way.

Jabarie whistled. "Damn! You got some serious issues, huh?"

"Yeah, I think you bowl better when you're distracted," Jace said with a laugh.

Diamere glared over at his cousins before returning to his seat.

"That sexy little female wouldn't have anything to do with your mood, would she?" Jace asked with a raised eyebrow. "What was her name?"

"Kelly," Jabarie chimed in as he prepared to bowl.

At the mention of her name, Diamere lowered his gaze to his plastic cup. She had everything to do with what he was feeling. How could a woman have become so important to him?

"Now I think we're getting somewhere," Jaden stated as he slid over on the bench.

After bowling a seven, Jabarie returned to his seat. "Man, take it from me. If you want her, then don't let anything stand in the way."

Diamere met Jabarie's intense look and knew that he was talking from personal experience. He had lost Brenna when his meddling parents tried to intervene. Their interference cost the couple five years of misery before they finally found each other again.

"I agree," Jaden added. "You know I almost lost Danica because of something that was said. Take it from me, it's not worth it."

Diamere dragged a hand across his face. He had been in denial for the past few weeks but couldn't lie to himself any longer. He hadn't seen Kelly in three days and he had a deep pain inside that only she could mend. He had to come to terms with what had happened. And he was now ready to admit that he loved her. There was no way he could keep playing this game. His cousins were right—it was time for him to go get his woman.

Chapter 19

This is just what I needed, Kelly thought as she stood on the sunporch where she had spent so much of her life, staring out at the lake in front of her. A satisfied smile softened her mouth. Her grandparents' cottage was located in a secluded wooded section of Rehoboth Beach, on a cul-de-sac with four other houses. The stretch of private lake was shared only by the homes that surrounded it. At one time the water used to be stocked with fish, but her grandfather said it hadn't been that way in over a decade.

For as long as she could remember, Kelly had spent all her summers here—the times when she left the world of reality behind to enter one of sheer fantasy. And fantasy was what it was going to take to get her to stop thinking about Diamere.

She took a seat on a padded patio lounge chair and picked up a book that had been highly recommended by Essence. But after an hour of comparing the hero in the story to Diamere, Kelly groaned and tossed the book aside. Staring out at the lake again, she felt a tidal wave of emotion wash over her. She was definitely in love, and not being with Diamere, not being able to see his handsome face, caused a painful ache inside. She was beginning to think that maybe she had simply been in love with the idea of being in love. Had to be. She had gotten over Devin way too easily. None of his gifts or begging her to take him back had swayed her decision to end their relationship. Yet with Diamere it was different, she thought as she brought her iced tea to her lips and tried to swallow down the lump in her throat. Losing Diamere, she felt as if she had also lost a part of herself.

She rose from the chair and wandered to the other end of the deck, leaning against the railing. They'd had an understanding. A no-strings-attached relationship. Neither of them wanted a commitment. Or did they? Her breath stilled as she considered the question carefully. Being his wife… Giving birth to his children… Her heart skipped a beat just thinking about being Mrs. Diamere Redmond. Mother and wife. Children with his smooth chocolate skin and her large cinnamon eyes… Unconsciously, she placed her hand over her stomach. Was there any chance that maybe—

Realizing she was being ridiculous, she pushed that thought aside, as well. What they had was a short, end-of-summer fling that was now over. No matter how desperately she wanted him.

She closed her eyes again and willed away thoughts of him. School was starting next week and she was going to be too busy meeting her darling little students and teaching them how to count and read to have time for a relationship. Yep. It was a good thing their fling had run its course and was finally over.

The sun had begun to beat down on her face. Feeling sticky, Kelly slid open the patio door and stepped into the house, where she was met by a gust of cool air. Her damp shirt turned cold, and immediately she began to shiver. Kelly moved to her room and pulled a T-shirt from a drawer just as her cell phone beeped, indicating a missed call. Picking it up, she checked first to see who had called. Essence. Five times.

She hit Talk and waited until her sister-in-law picked up on the other line.

"Why haven't you called us!" she barked by way of greeting.

Kelly's lips twitched with humor. "Sorry. I was wrapped up in the beauty of this place and forgot all about phoning."

"Well, your mother is worried sick."

She rolled her eyes dramatically. "My mother forgets I am a grown woman."

"You're not *that* grown," Essence replied with a snort. "And you know, regardless of how old you get, you'll always be your mother's baby."

She chuckled and held the phone to her ear with one hand while she pulled her shirt over her head with the other. "You're definitely right about that. I'll give her a call later to let her know I'm okay."

"You better." There was a slight pause. "Somebody's been asking about you."

Her head rose. "Who?"

"You know who."

Kelly knew but she needed to hear Essence say it.

"Come on, Kelly, you know it's Diamere."

She clicked her tongue. "What's he want?"

"He came over here last night, and he and Mark were in the living room for a long time, talking. I tried to eavesdrop, but as soon as I stepped through the door they both stopped talking. But I know they were talking about you."

Kelly snorted through the phone. "They could have been talking about baseball."

"Nope. Because as I was going to the kitchen, Diamere stopped me and asked if you had made it safely. I told him you did, but I wouldn't know since you hadn't bothered to call anyone."

Kelly smiled at the thought that Diamere had been asking about her. Still, she needed to stay focused. "I hope you didn't tell him where to find me."

"Of course not. I know you need your space. But that's not to say Mark didn't run his mouth. There's no telling."

Oh, brother. The last thing she needed was for Mark to give away her hiding place. "I hope he didn't."

"Diamere looked really sad that you were no longer here."

She gave a weak laugh as she lowered herself onto the bed. "Oh, please. It's not like he'll never see me again."

"No, but he looked like he knew what the two of you had was over."

"It *is* over between us. Diamere isn't interested in anything other than a fling. Well, I ain't the one."

There was a pause. "But I thought that was what you wanted."

Kelly released a heavy sigh. "It was, or at least that's

what I thought I wanted. But once I started seeing Diamere, I realized I wanted something more." She wanted everything love had to offer. The house with the white picket fence and the two-plus kids. She was even willing to give up her Saturn for a family minivan.

"Can I ask you a question?"

Kelly groaned. "Even if I say no you're gonna ask me anyway."

"True." Essence chuckled, then immediately sobered. "Do you love him?"

"Yes," she said breathlessly. "I never stopped loving him." She had finally come to terms with it. Diamere had always held her heart.

"Have you told him?"

"Are you crazy? Hell no."

"Well, why not?" her sister-in-law said, as if the solution was simple.

"Diamere made it clear that he wasn't looking for anything serious, so what would I look like, telling him I loved him?"

"You might find out he feels the same way."

Her breathing stalled. "Does he?"

"I don't know. That's something you need to find out for yourself. You owe it to yourself."

Kelly flopped back on the bed. "Listen, I already put my heart on the line once. There is no way I'm setting myself up for another letdown. If Diamere wants me for more than a quick romp in the sack, then he needs to let me know. Otherwise the relationship is over."

Essence released a heavy sigh in her ear. "I don't know who's more stubborn, you or Mark."

Kelly chuckled. "I think I've got him beat."

"I'm beginning to agree."

They chatted for a while longer, then said their goodbyes. Moving down to the kitchen, Kelly thought about what Essence had said. There was no way she would ever tell Diamere she loved him. What they had was over and the sooner her heart realized that the better.

Chapter 20

After dinner, Kelly sat out on the deck reading again. The temperature had cooled off considerably and she appreciated the breeze. The weatherman called for heavy rain in the morning and the rest of the week. Kelly frowned. It was just what she needed to darken her mood.

She glanced into the pale water, which gleamed invitingly, its promise of coolness irresistible to her heated flesh. A swim might help her get to sleep tonight, she thought. And if it was expected to rain for the duration of her visit, this evening might be her last chance.

Rising, she went inside and changed into a pink-and-white bathing suit. She slid her feet into a pair of white flip-flops and went into the bathroom to retrieve a towel. Within minutes she was at the dock, where her grandfather kept a small boat. Kelly lowered her towel onto the wood planks and waded into the lake. Once clear of the edges, which were choked with weeds, she swam for about a hundred yards. The water was cool and invigorating. When she reached the center of the lake, Kelly turned over and floated on her back and closed her eyes. Immediately, images of Diamere danced before her and her body ached for his touch. She missed him. There was no denying it. He had made her feel alive and every bit a woman. In such a short time he had showed her how wrong she had been. There was still love in her heart and a part of her was still willing to give it another chance, with the hope of eventually finding the man she would one day spend the rest of her life with. How ironic that she'd found that in the one man she couldn't have.

Tears stung the corners of her eyes, rolled down her cheeks and into the lake. Getting over Diamere was not going to be easy; she could see that now. She also knew she had made the right choice by ending their relationship the way she had. She was in too deep and any further involvement would have done nothing but intensify the heartache.

She wasn't sure how long she lay there thinking about him and the time they'd spent together, before she heard a bird crying overhead.

Brushing Diamere from her mind, Kelly flipped over onto her stomach and swam several feet before she stopped for a brief rest and noticed that clouds had accumulated. The sky had grown strangely gray. She had swum at night many times growing up. When her grandparents weren't paying attention, she would sneak out of her room for a swim. It was her time alone, without her brother underfoot. A time for her own private thoughts. However, this evening the silence seemed unusually eerie, making her feel apprehensive. She glanced around and noticed none of the neighbors were sitting out on their decks. Everything was quiet, except for the wind, which had begun to pick up speed. Feeling increasingly uneasy, Kelly started swimming back toward the dock. A moment later she knew she had made the right choice when the skies were suddenly split by a bright flash of lightning.

A storm. She had never been out in the lake during a storm before. Whenever one struck at the cottage she always had fun curling up under the covers between her grandparents, holding a small flashlight. But she wasn't in her grandparents' bed. She was out in the middle of the lake. Suddenly frightened, she swam faster, while rumbles of thunder increased as the storm drew nearer. The sky lit up as another flash of lightning danced over the water, making her conscious of her own safety.

Kelly was close to the pier when thunder clapped loudly as a tree was struck by a bolt of lightning. It was a large oak and it came down with a crash. Kelly saw it falling, but she was too much in shock to move. At the last moment she swam to the side and the tree missed her, but the waves from it engulfed her, nearly drowning her as they swept her under. Half blinded by fear, she didn't see the man cutting through the water in her direction with swift, powerful strokes.

Spluttering wildly, Kelly tried to fight her way back to the surface, but the waves were too much for her. Her arms and legs hurt and she was suddenly so tired she gasped for breath. She must have lost consciousness and started to dream, because she felt arms around her, lifting her out of the water. It took her a few seconds to realize that the face she saw and the voice she heard belonged to Diamere.

"Kelly, quit fighting me! I got you. Just hold still!"

His tone was raspy, almost as much so as his breathing. Realizing he had her safe, Kelly quit flailing and allowed him to carry her. She knew if she didn't they would both drown. Holding on to her, he swam to the shore and lifted her from the water. Clinging to him, she choked helplessly as she tried to clear her lungs. When Diamere reached the pier, he stretched her out on the wooden planks. She lay there coughing and spitting up water as her heart pounded.

Diamere climbed out of the water. Immediately, he cradled her in his arms and gazed down at her. Fear and concern burned in his eyes. "Baby, are you okay?"

She was glad he was here. If he hadn't come when he had, there was no telling what might have happened. "Yes, I'm okay," she managed to say after clearing her lungs some more. The rain beat heavily on her face and skin, yet the feeling was refreshing considering what had just happened to her. Diamere stroked her shoulder as he tried to bring his own breathing under control. "What in the world were you thinking, swimming on a night like this?"

"It wasn't raining when I set out," she gasped, then coughed some more.

Diamere lifted her into his arms and she rested her cheek against his chest as he carried her away from the lake and up the path toward the cottage. She didn't know how he knew which house belonged to her grandparents or what he was doing here, but right now she was too exhausted to care. She was just glad he was here. Closing her eyes, she tightened her hold around his neck while the rain continued to fall.

Diamere carried her through the door and into the bedroom, where he sat her down on the bed, helping her out of her bathing suit. Kelly was too tired to object. Her arms were so heavy she could barely lift them. As soon as she was completely undressed, he reached for her grandmother's handmade quilt and wrapped it around Kelly's shivering body, then assisted her to lie down on the bed.

"Don't move. I'll be right back."

At his instruction, she waited as he went out through the door and down the hall. Within seconds she heard water pouring into the tub.

Rain was still beating heavily on the roof and lightning flashed outside of the bedroom window. Kelly began to shiver uncontrollably, not because she was cold but because she was scared. What in the world had she been thinking, going swimming when a thunderstorm was coming? If her family ever found out, she would never hear the end of it. She would have to swear Diamere to secrecy.

Kelly was too exhausted to think straight, but she was almost certain the sky was only slightly overcast when she had first headed out. The meteorologist had predicted rain wasn't due until late evening. So what happened? She took a deep breath. It wouldn't be the first time a weatherman was wrong. Forecasting was more like fortune-telling.

Closing her eyes, she relaxed on the bed. If Diamere hadn't arrived just then, there was no telling what might have happened.

Nope, she wasn't going to go there. She pushed the

thought aside and thanked the Lord for delivering her through an incident that could have been tragic.

She'd started to drift off to sleep when she felt someone tapping her on the arm. "Kelly, wake up."

Slowly, she raised her eyelids and groaned. "No. Let me sleep, please."

"Not until I'm sure you're okay. Look at you. You're still shivering." He tossed back the blanket and lifted her out of the bed as if she were a small child, then carried her down the hall to the bathroom.

With stubborn pride, Kelly pushed against his chest. "Diamere, I c-c-can walk!" she cried, teeth chattering.

"Hush, Kelly. I need to get you warm," he commanded gently, with enough deep tones in his voice that she knew it wasn't up for discussion. Once he stepped into the bathroom he lowered her gently into the tub of warm water. Any further protest evaporated instantly. "Lie back and relax," he said as he took a seat on the floor next to the tub.

Kelly gave him a curious glance. "Are you going to sit there and watch me?"

His mouth quirked. "I've already seen you naked."

She blushed and looked down, realizing she was completely exposed. "Just because you've seen me doesn't mean I want an audience."

"I'll stay just long enough to know you're okay."

After a couple of seconds, she gave him a nonchalant shrug. "Suit yourself."

Ignoring him, she leaned back and slid beneath the water. Within minutes her body temperature rose and she started to feel herself relaxing. Closing her eyes, she released a heavy sigh.

"Sounds like you're feeling better already."

She opened her eyes and gave him a sidelong look. "I am, thanks."

He smiled and appeared pleased that she was going to be okay. "How about some tea?"

Her eyelids fluttered open long enough for her to look up at him. Did he really care that much? "Tea sounds wonderful." Her eyes traveled the length of his wet body. "You might want to check the room across the hall. Mark should have something dry you can put on."

Nodding, Diamere rose from the floor and headed down the hall in search of the kitchen. As Kelly closed her eyes, a thought suddenly came to her mind. What in the world was he doing here?

Diamere went into the kitchen and combed the cabinets until he found the tea bags and a large blue mug. Moving to the sink, he filled the mug to the rim with water, then walked over to the utility cart near the window and popped the microwave open, setting the mug inside. While he waited for the water to heat, he paced around the room, trying to keep his emotions under control.

Kelly could have drowned. His hands began to shake and his chest filled with overwhelming fear. He had never been so scared in his life. His mind traveled back to those moments leading up to discovering her kicking and screaming in the lake. He had pulled up to the house and, finding the door unlocked, had walked in and called her name. He'd happened to be in the kitchen, looking for her out back, when he noticed something in the lake beyond. The rain was coming down too hard for him to see clearly, so he had stepped out onto the back porch, and just as he reached the top step he had heard her scream.

He'd jumped into action. Chest pounding with fear, he'd rushed down the hill and dived into the water.

He smoothed a hand across his face and forced himself to take a deep breath. What would he have done if he had lost her? He shook that thought aside as he removed the mug and dropped the tea bag inside. He wasn't going to let himself think about it.

He loved her. He took a deep breath as the realization of just how much he loved her hit him. He loved her so much that he would have drowned trying to save her life. Did she know how special she was to him? Of course not. Because he had been too stupid to tell her just how much she truly meant to him. He had almost let her walk out of his life. Well, he had come to his senses and there was no way he was leaving without letting her know just how much he cared.

Diamere took a saucer from the cabinet, set the mug on it and reached for a spoon and the sugar bowl, and carried both back down the hall to the bathroom. He was disappointed to see Kelly was no longer there.

"The water started to get cold, so I thought it would be smart to get dressed and get in bed."

He noticed that she had found the red-and-navy flannel robe that had been hanging on the back of the bathroom door, and had slipped it on.

"Why don't you get under the covers?" he suggested.

Kelly stuck her chin out defiantly. "I'm not a baby."

"I didn't say you were," he told her quietly.

She looked as if she was about to say something,

but thought better of it and instead went to the bed and slipped beneath the covers. "Satisfied?"

"Very," he replied with a grin as he moved over and took a seat beside her.

Kelly took the tea from his hand and stirred in two teaspoons of sugar, then brought the warm liquid to her lips.

"I'm going to go find something dry to put on." He rose and leaned over and pressed his lips against hers.

As he headed for the door, Kelly called after him, "Thank you for saving my life."

"You're welcome. Now get some rest." He turned and went to Mark's room across the hall to find something dry, while Kelly finished her tea.

After taking a shower and putting on dry clothes, Diamere checked on Kelly. She had drifted off to sleep. He crawled into bed beside her, pressed a kiss to her disheveled hair and tightened his arm around her. This was his woman. Kelly belonged to him. A wave of protectiveness surged over him. He was willing to lose his own life to keep her safe. He would never let her go.

Chapter 21

Kelly opened her eyes and allowed herself time to adjust to gray light coming in through the windows. Rain was still beating down heavily outside and she released a sigh. She was in the country vacationing and didn't have anywhere to go this morning, so there was no rush to get up. With another sigh, she shut her eyes again and snuggled into the covers.

She'd started to drift off to sleep once more when she suddenly bolted upright. *Diamere.* Her heart began to thump in her chest. He was somewhere in the cottage. Tossing the covers aside, she rose from the bed and slipped her feet into her pale blue slippers. As she moved down the hall, she tightened the belt on her robe. When she reached the kitchen she stopped in her tracks.

"Good morning, beautiful." Diamere greeted her with a warm smile, then reached for a spatula and flipped a golden-brown pancake.

"Hi," she replied in a voice filled with uncertainty. She was in awe at the kind man before her. The smells of fresh coffee and bacon mingled in the air.

After a moment of silence, he glanced over at her and asked, "How'd you sleep?"

"Fine," she replied as she crossed the room and took a seat at the table.

"Good. I thought about waking you but I figured after what you went through you needed your rest."

Her eyes traveled to the apple-shaped clock on the wall and she gasped. "It's almost ten o'clock."

He nodded. "I know. I checked in on you at eight just to make sure you were still breathing," he replied with a hint of amusement.

He met her eyes and stared at her for a long moment before she turned away and self-consciously combed her fingers through her hair. Why was he here? she wondered. Diamere still hadn't told her. Not that she had given him a chance.

"Ready for some coffee?" he asked, breaking into her thoughts. Kelly nodded, then watched him reach for a mug and fill it. She couldn't help admiring how good he looked in his low-rise denim jeans and a simple black T-shirt that strained across his massive biceps. His feet were bare and she realized how comfortable and at home he looked.

Kelly gazed out the window. Rain was still beating steadily against the glass. It was a summer storm like none she had ever seen. For the moment it seemed as if they were stranded out here at the lake. Thank goodness school didn't start for another week. Mama Tate was a smart woman, and with the grocery store being so far away, she always kept the cottage freezer stocked with food.

"Is the power out?"

Diamere nodded. "Yep. Thank goodness you have a generator, so we at least have lights, but the phones don't work. I think that big tree cut the power line." He turned to her and the corner of his mouth twitched upward. "So in other words, we're stranded."

Realization sank in. The two of them were alone together until the storm was over. Kelly's heart pounded heavily at the prospect of being alone with him for any amount of time.

Diamere carried over her coffee along with a plate, and placed them on the table in front of her. Kelly looked down at the food, then back up at him. "Aren't you going to eat, too?"

He filled his mug, then headed to the table and took a seat. "I've already eaten."

Kelly shrugged, then reluctantly reached for a knife and fork and cut into the fluffy stack.

"It's beautiful out here. I can see why you like to come," he murmured.

She nodded and finished chewing. "I've loved this place all my life."

Diamere looked out the window. Silence hung in the room for several minutes.

"Why are you here?" she finally asked.

He avoided making eye contact, reaching over to her plate and stealing a slice of bacon. "I'll tell you later. Right now I want to know why you were out in that water."

His question was simple enough. She shrugged. "I already told you. I felt like swimming."

"Didn't you know a storm was on the way?"

Kelly took a sip of coffee as she thought about his question. "Yes, but I wasn't expecting it to happen until much later. When I noticed the sky had gotten dark I tried to get back, but it was too late."

"Why were you swimming so late in the evening?"

"You sure ask a lot of questions," she said wryly.

"I'm just trying to understand."

She narrowed her gaze. "Why? So you can tell Mark on me?"

"Yeah, as a matter of fact. Maybe he'll talk some sense into you so you won't do something so stupid again. You could have drowned."

"Stupid?" she repeated. Diamere sure had a lot of nerve. "Stupid as you coming all the way down here? Now I'm stuck with you until the storm clears!"

Diamere took a sip from his mug, then rose. "Actually, coming here was the smartest decision I've ever made." He leaned in and pressed his lips to hers, catching Kelly completely off guard. "Now that I know you're okay, I'm going to grab my bag out of the car and take a shower." He walked off, whistling a tune.

The wonderful breakfast was stuck in Kelly's throat. As long as he kissed her like that, she was far from okay. Hearing the front door shut, she stepped to the window and watched him go out to his SUV and retrieve a black duffel bag. He had come here with the intention of staying.

A warm feeling flooded her body. What was he up to?

She continued to think about it as she finished her breakfast and started on the dishes. From down the hall she could hear the sound of running water, and couldn't help thinking about Diamere standing under the warm spray of the shower in all his naked glory.

The last time she'd seen him was after they had made love, after leaving Hadley. She had made it clear, or at least she thought she had, that she was not at all interested in continuing their relationship. Kelly's blood began to boil. She hoped he hadn't come out here to persuade her to do otherwise. Diamere was stubborn; she knew that for a fact. But if he thought he was going to get his way this time, he was in for a rude awakening.

Lightning flashed outside the window again and the rumble of thunder made her shudder. Hearing the shower water turn off, she decided to go confront Diamere. But he wasn't in the bathroom. After searching all three bedrooms, to no avail, she moved down the oak wood hallway to the spacious family room at the back of the house, where she found him searching the built-in wall unit.

"What are you doing?" she asked, standing in the doorway with her hands on her hips.

Diamere swung around and she looked down at the board game in his hands. "Care for a round of Scrabble?"

"Scrabble?" she asked, brow lowered in confusion. "No, I don't want to play. What I want is to know why you're here."

"I'll tell you what. You beat me at a game of Scrabble, and I'll tell you whatever you want." Kelly didn't miss the glint of a challenge sparkling in Diamere's eyes.

A smiled curled her lips. If there was one thing she was good at, it was Scrabble. She would have her questions answered in no time.

* * *

An hour later, Kelly was frustrated—sexually frustrated.

"Kelly, is something wrong?" Diamere asked as he watched her mop her forehead for what he figured was probably the seventh or eighth time.

"No, I'm fine. Just hurry up."

He placed his letters on the board, and when she looked down, she did exactly what he had spelled: m-o-a-n.

Kelly was frustrated, all right. Every word Diamere spelled had some romantic meaning. *Sex. Lips. Kiss. Wet.* And now *moan.* What in the world was he up to?

"It's your turn."

"Yeah, yeah, I know," she snapped, feeling increasingly irritated by the second. She didn't have much to choose from.

"Are you going to finish playing or what?" he taunted.

"Just give me a minute," she growled. The game was supposed to have been a simple slam dunk. Instead, he was beating her badly. She still had five letters left, while he only had one. Nibbling her lower lip, she studied the board, and then a smile curled her lips. She reached for three letters and added them to a letter *Y,* to spell out *play.*

"Play, huh?"

"Yeah, like we're playing a game of Scrabble because someone is trying to play games instead of telling me why he's here." She rolled her eyes and reached for a bottle of water.

Diamere's face creased with laughter. "No games. I told you I'd tell you if you win." A smirk took over his expression. "Unfortunately, though, I got this game in the bag."

With a look of amusement, he picked up the last tile chip from his tray and set it on the board, spelling *sexy*. "Sweetheart, that's what you are to me. Sexy."

His words caused the churning in her stomach to intensify. Every time his gaze met hers, her heart turned over in response. Kelly caught herself moistening her lips as he leaned in close enough to kiss her. Instead of doing so, he whispered in her ear, "Looks like I get to keep my secret a little longer."

She pulled back with a furious gasp. He was getting a big kick out of teasing her.

"How about double or nothing?" he challenged.

With a frown, she rose from her chair. "How about I'm tired and I'm going to go read my book. The thing I had planned to do before you interrupted my vacation."

He rose, as well. "While you're reading, I'm going to work on that leaky sink in the kitchen." He packed up the game and returned it to the shelf.

Kelly shook her head in disbelief. "You really aren't going to tell me, are you?"

"I will. Just not yet." He cupped her chin and pressed his lips to hers, then headed toward the kitchen.

Kelly was livid. How dare he think he could drive down to the lake and seduce her into continuing his no-frills relationship? Well, he had another thing coming. The only thing stopping her from throwing him out was the storm raging around them. Furiously, she stalked down the hall to her room and flopped onto the bed.

Refusing to waste another second thinking about him, she reached for the book on the nightstand and opened to the page she had bookmarked. Within minutes she was into the story, and found herself wrapped up in the love affair between the two main characters. Kelly couldn't help but wonder why love was so perfect in books, and was thinking of every reason why it wasn't possible to be that way in real life when she felt her eyelids grow heavy. With a yawn, she curled up into the pillows and drifted off to sleep.

Diamere found what he was looking for, then closed the door to the shed out back and headed into the house. Replacing the worn washer was an easy enough job, and gave him the excuse he had needed to put some distance between himself and Kelly.

A smile curled his lips as he thought about the expression on her lovely face as he'd teased her. He felt that she had been seconds away from asking him to leave, which was why he'd decided to get out of her way. Not that it would have mattered. With the rain coming down the way it was, he was certain the bridge at the end of the road was washed out.

He reached for a wrench and within minutes had the leak stopped and the faucet back in working order. There was no noise coming from down the hall, and Diamere was beginning to wonder if maybe he had pushed her too far. He loved Kelly and had every intention of telling her just that, but he was going to do it on his own time. He was still getting used to the idea, and part of him, his pride, wanted to know if she felt the same way about him. *What if she didn't?* The possibility kept running through his head, especially while they were playing Scrabble, and she'd grown angry and mentioned she wasn't too happy about him ruining her vacation. The sooner he told her how he felt, the better for both of them, because he wasn't sure how much more either of them could take.

Chapter 22

Kelly yawned and glanced out the window. The rain was still coming down, but had slowed up a bit. Hearing movement coming from the front of the house, she rolled her eyes toward the ceiling. They were stuck here together. There was nothing either of them could do about it until the storm had passed. Reluctantly, she rose from bed and headed down the hall to the bathroom. She was tempted to hide out in her room until morning. The way things looked outside, she was almost certain the storm would be over by then and the roads would be manageable.

After brushing her teeth and running a comb through her hair, Kelly moved down the hall and into the kitchen. Entering the room, she found Diamere looking inside the refrigerator. He lifted his head and greeted her with a smile.

"I was planning to grill the salmon you had in the

refrigerator, unless you would rather have something else."

She shook her head. "No, salmon sounds good. But it's raining outside."

He shrugged. "I'll pull the grill under the awning. It won't take that long to fix fish."

"You're the boss. Do you need some help?"

"How about you make a salad?"

"I'm on it."

While she washed the lettuce and chopped vegetables, he went outside and fired up the barbecue. From the kitchen window she watched him. He had taken off his shirt and was wearing a plain white T-shirt that showed off his muscular arms and the tight muscles of his stomach. *Stop looking at him.* All she was doing was making matters worse.

As soon as she finished preparing an attractive-looking salad, she grabbed a bottle of wine from the top shelf of the refrigerator and carried both out onto the sunporch. By the time she got the cork out, Diamere was coming through the door with the grilled salmon.

"Perfect timing," she said as she stared down at the main course.

"I told you it would take no time." He set the plate down on the table next to the salad, then pulled his wet T-shirt over his head. Her gaze dropped to his chest and traveled over the dark mat of hair, now wet from the rain. "Let me go and wash up so we can eat," he added.

Kelly watched him leave the room, admiring his walk and the way his blue jeans hugged his perfect butt. *Oh, boy.* The next several hours were not going to be easy.

The rain had slowed and the sky had turned an

orange-red. She managed to take a moment away from her racing thoughts to appreciate the beauty of their surroundings.

The two of them were relatively quiet as they ate. She was trying to patiently wait until Diamere decided to tell her the reason for his visit, and instead of getting angry again, she decided it was best just to act as if she didn't care one way or the other.

"It looks like the rain is slowing," he said, to break the silence.

Chewing her food, she nodded. "Yes, it is, finally."

"Hopefully, tomorrow I'll be able to return home."

Why did she suddenly feel saddened at the thought of him leaving, especially since she had made it clear he had interrupted her vacation? "Yes, you probably will."

There was a pregnant pause before he asked, "When are you returning home?"

She stared across the table at his beautiful chocolate eyes. "Not until Saturday. School starts on Monday, and I want to enjoy the weekend because I won't get another time to relax like this until Christmas break."

"Are you looking forward to the semester starting?" he asked between bites of salmon.

"I can't wait." She couldn't help the excitement in her voice.

"What is it you like so much about teaching?"

Kelly met Diamere's eyes and could tell he was actually interested in listening to her talk about her job.

"I like it when my students' faces light up when they've learned something new. Nothing warms my heart more than that." While they ate, she went on to talk about the class of students she'd had the year before. Kelly loved the way Diamere listened and only interrupted when he had a question. Devin had never wanted to talk about the students after hours.

"I can tell you truly love your job. That's important," Diamere said when she finally finished.

She nodded. "I do. I really do."

He took a sip of wine, then licked his lips. She found herself following the swipe of his tongue with her eyes.

"I know Nana asked you this, but do you really see yourself having kids of your own someday?" he asked at last.

She nodded. "Yes, I definitely want children. I think some women are meant to be mothers, and I'm sure I'm one of them."

"I agree. I think you would make an excellent mother."

"And you would make an excellent father." Kelly wanted to mention Ryan's daughters, but decided against it.

Diamere looked over at her, his eyes serious. "I didn't think I would be any good at being a father, but when the twins were born I fell in love with them so fast there wasn't anything I wouldn't do for my angels. I…" His voice broke and he reached for his glass and took another drink.

Kelly's stomach turned. It had been over a year, yet the pain was still there. She placed a comforting hand on his arm. "I know it's still hard."

He nodded. "It is. Someday I hope to have kids again."

"I know you'll be a fabulous father."

Their eyes met and her heart flipped as she saw his sadness. "You think so?"

She nodded and couldn't stop the tears that filled her eyes. "I know so."

"Hearing that makes me so sure about what I'm going to do."

Kelly licked her lips. "What is that?"

"Kiss you." Diamere leaned forward slightly and took the flute from her hand, setting it back on the table. His other hand slid around her neck, gliding smoothly over her skin. Excitement stirred within her, and her lips parted as he drew closer and his lips brushed hers. Diamere rose from his chair, bringing Kelly with him without breaking the kiss. He wound an arm around her waist and pulled her tight against him.

"I want you. I couldn't go another night without you," he confessed. He crushed his mouth over hers, kissing her deeply.

Kelly accepted what he offered. She wrapped her arms around his neck and met his tongue stroke for stroke, her lips softening under his.

"Why are you here?" she asked again.

"For you. I came here to be with you." He caressed her breast through the sundress and squeezed her nipple between his thumb and forefinger, arousing her. How in the world did she think she could live without this? Her body ached for his touch, and to her relief he moved his hand to her other breast.

"But why?" she asked, growing irritated by his lack of words, though simultaneously aroused by the exploration of his hands.

"I can show you better than I can tell you," he groaned before his tongue again explored the recesses of her mouth. "I can't fight it any longer. You're like a drug I've become addicted to."

He drew her dress up her knee and slid his hand underneath, pushing her panties to the side and making room for his hand.

"Spread your legs."

Eagerly, Kelly parted her thighs and moaned as his finger slid inside her wetness. "Diamere," she cried out, her trembling limbs clinging to him.

"That's right. Say my name," he growled, thrusting another finger into her wet heat. Kelly shuddered, her entire body waiting for this moment. Her desire for him was too overwhelming to ignore. Any attempt to stop what was happening was a waste of time. She was lost in the feel of his fingers stroking her in the most intimate way. "You miss me touching you like this, don't you?"

"Diamere!" she cried. It took everything she had not to collapse to her knees. He increased the pressure and spread her thighs wider. Kelly found herself rocking her hips to the rhythm of his fingers. It wasn't long before her body clamped down hard against his penetration and she shuddered with pleasure. "Yes, yes," she moaned as she rode the final wave. She waited until her breathing resumed before she looked up shyly, filled with confusion about what was happening between them. The smoldering flame she saw in his eyes startled her.

"You are so beautiful when you come apart in my arms." With that he lowered his head and seared a path down the column of her neck, across her racing pulse beating heavily beneath her skin. He lifted her off her feet and carried her over to the table. "Lie back."

Kelly complied, resting her weight on her elbows

and her feet on the table. Diamere slid her panties down past her knees, over her ankles and onto the floor, then pushed her thighs apart. He looked at her and she was sure he saw desire burning in her eyes just before he lowered his head. On contact, she practically jumped off the table. The feel of his tongue between her legs brought her to life. "Please…" She closed her eyes and moaned.

He increased the pressure and circled the bud with the smooth tip of his tongue in a way she had only dreamed of a man doing. Then he spread her wider and settled his mouth even deeper between her thighs. She let out a moan as he buried his tongue inside her and stroked her with long sweeps. His teasing touch had her arching into his mouth while she gripped the back of his head and pulled him closer. He nipped and suckled her as he dipped into her sweetness.

Kelly was burning with need. It was obvious this was another game to him. He wanted her begging for him. All she wanted was to feel him inside her body, with his hips pumping furiously to bring them both pleasure. She looked up to see him staring down at her as he loosened his pants, reached for a condom in his pocket and slid it on. Those few seconds felt like forever.

"Shift your hips toward me."

She slid her trembling body off the table and Diamere wrapped her legs around his waist, preventing her from falling.

"I can't wait to be inside of you." He slipped his hand between her legs. "Damn, you're wet." He settled himself there and lifted her bottom in the palms of his hands.

Her eyes glazed over as he positioned himself and

slid inside. Kelly exhaled on contact and tightened her muscles possessively around him. He groaned and was soon trembling for control, obviously trying to take his time and make the moment last as long as possible.

"Diamere," she breathed. She arched against him, her hands gripping his waist, then cupping his buttocks, urging him deeper still. "I want all of you, Diamere."

His response was immediate. In one swift movement, he buried himself completely, grunting with the effort. Kelly cried out in pleasure and clamped down on him hard.

"I can't seem to get enough of you. Nothing has ever felt this good," he panted.

His words were like music to her ears. Still, she knew he was caught up in the euphoria of the moment, and his words would be meaningless later. She bit back the thought and focused on the pleasure he was bringing her.

Diamere turned her face to his. He brushed his mouth against her parted lips. "You're mine, Kelly. Make no mistake," he said as he pumped his hips, and she welcomed every thrust into her body with a fervor that shook her to her very soul.

"Tell me you're mine."

How could she ever forget how completely he fulfilled her? How complete she felt when they were together? "I'm yours." Today, tomorrow, for as long as he wanted, she was his. Tears burned the backs of her eyes. Who was she trying to fool? There was no way she could have ended their affair. Not until it had run its course, and she parted with a broken heart. Diamere had become too important to her and she just wasn't ready to let that go yet.

His heart pounded as she held him close, cradling his muscled body against her own. She wanted to keep him inside of her forever.

"You're mine," he said.

"Yes," she answered. "Yes, I'm yours."

"Kelly? Look at me."

She opened her eyes and gazed at him, into dark eyes so tender and mesmerizing she was at a loss for words. His rhythm slowed between her thighs as he stared back at her.

"I want to tell you why I am here."

Kelly felt the air surrounding them sizzle with awareness.

"Before I walk out of your life forever, before I let you go once and for all, I have to tell to you something." She saw a muscle in his jaw tick as he fought for control.

"What's that?" she asked, hanging on to every word as the tension in the room increased.

"I love you, Kelly."

She blinked twice and gasped. Did she hear him right? "What did you say?"

Diamere pressed his mouth to hers in a slow, sensual dance, then pulled back and reaffirmed, "I said I love you."

His words were music to her ears, but in the heat of the moment a man was likely to say anything. She read enough issues of *Essence* magazine to know that. However, right now she didn't care.

She opened her legs wide and leaned forward, trailing her tongue across his neck and shoulder, and moaning at the taste of him. He rocked his hips, penetrating her deeper than she could ever have imagined. Her pleasure built steadily, sweeping her into a world of blissful sensation. Nothing had ever felt so good and nothing else ever would. She had to enjoy every second of what he was giving her because it would be their last. She felt herself spinning beyond rational thought, caught up in the rapture of their bodies joined as one.

"We belong together," he growled.

Her breath caught at his words. As his rhythm increased, her breath came out in a long, pleasured sigh. He was thick and hard and filled her completely.

"Kelly," he groaned, thrusting furiously, "I can't hold on… Kelly, I love you."

And then she was on fire and he was pumping so hard he had her crying out in pleasure as her body surrendered to him. She gave in to the delicious heat that had her convulsing in his arms.

Diamere grunted and let out a violent roar of release, his body tensing and then collapsing.

Kelly woke with the sheets tangled around her legs. She pulled them up over her body and found the satin material was scented with the musk of sex. She inhaled deeply, loving the delicious reminder of making love all night. She grinned as she stretched her sore muscles. It was worth it. After they'd made love on the table, Diamere had carried her back to the bedroom for a sensational night of passion.

Sunlight was peeking through the blinds in a clear indication that the rain had stopped, and the roads would be navigable again. The thought of their time together ending and Diamere going back home caused her to feel sick. Deep down she didn't want their time ever to end.

Curious where Diamere had wandered off to, Kelly

sat up in the bed and listened, but heard nothing. Slipping from the sheets, she went to the oak dresser and found a pink T-shirt and cutoff blue jeans shorts to put on. She dressed, then stepped into the bathroom and washed her face and brushed her teeth. Noticing her hair in the mirror, she reached for a soft-bristle brush and smoothed it back neatly, then slid on a headband.

The bedroom door opened and she turned as Diamere stepped into the room, carrying two cups of coffee.

"Good morning, sleepyhead," he said with a smile as he lowered the mugs onto the dresser. He then moved to where she was standing, and planted a kiss on her cheek.

Kelly took a deep breath, loving his clean masculine scent. "Diamere, we need to talk."

He nodded. "Yes, we do." He drew a deep breath in turn. "I shouldn't have said those things last night."

"You're right." *Oh, goodness. Here it comes.*

He gave her a considering glance. "That was not the time to tell someone you love them."

It took everything she had to hold her tears back. She had already understood he had said it in the heat of the moment. Didn't he know he was about to break her heart by reminding her?

"Please come and have a seat while I talk." Diamere took her hand and led her over to the bed. She lowered herself onto it, cupped her shaky hands in her lap and waited.

There was a serious glint in his eyes as he looked at her. "The last few weeks I've had some time to think. I realized I've made a lot of mistakes in my life, but there were things that happened that were out of my control. Unfortunately, I can't give up living and quit being who

I am because of it, and that was exactly what I was doing, putting a defensive wall up in order to keep my heart intact. I told you I wasn't interested in a serious relationship."

She quickly jumped in. "Yes, you did, and I'm okay—"

He put a finger to her lips, cutting her off. "Kelly, let me finish."

She wanted so desperately to tell him that it was okay, she knew he was just caught up in the moment. "Diamere, really, no apology is needed."

He combed a frustrated hand through his hair. "Woman! Can you please let your man finish, please?" She noticed the way his voice softened at the end. She also realized he had said "your man."

"Okay."

"Thank you." Reaching out, Diamere took her hand and stared down at her, looking more serious than she had ever seen him. "Kelly, my life is incomplete without you."

Her head sprang up. Had she heard him right? "What?"

His eyebrows furrowed. "Are you listening?"

"Of course I'm listening. Sorry, go ahead."

He smiled, then reached out and cupped her chin. "What I'm trying to say, Kelly, is that I love you. I want to be with you and only you, and see where that love leads us."

She stared at him with her mouth wide open. Diamere really did love her. Her heart was pounding.

"Kelly, do you hear me talking to you?"

She nodded her head as uncontrollable tears fell. "I hear you."

"Do you think you could ever consider giving us a chance? I should warn you that I refuse to take no for an answer. I plan to be at your school every day to take you to lunch, and at your doorstep, doing everything I can to prove to you I am a good man and we—"

This time Kelly pressed a finger to his lips. "Diamere, hush," she warned, then smiled. "Yes, I'm interested. I love you."

She noticed the way his eyes widened and his smile deepened. "Say that again."

"I said I love you, too, Diamere."

He kissed her gently, tenderly, his lips brushing the tears from her cheeks. Happiness and peace filled her.

"Oh, Diamere. I love you so much."

He kissed her lips with soft reverence, his eyes lit with love. "And I you." He drew her into his arms and lowered his mouth to hers. When he pulled back he met her warm smile. "Come on. I've got breakfast ready. Let's go eat and then afterward how about another game of Scrabble?"

"Don't you want to check the roads?"

He shook his head. "Nope. As far as I'm concerned, we're stranded here until it's time to head back on Saturday. And I can think of a couple of things we can do to help pass the time," he said with a devilish smile, before he leaned down and kissed her again. "I love you, Kelly."

Another tear slid down her cheek. She had never been so happy in her life. Together they walked toward the kitchen, and the rising sun she saw through the window seemed to symbolize the bright future that awaited them.

Epilogue

Kellis glanced around the Sheraton Beach Hotel grand ballroom at the crowd that had come to celebrate her marriage to Diamere Redmond. She turned around just as Essence came running over to her.

"You did it!" her friend yelled as she gathered Kelly in a hug. When she stepped back there were tears in her eyes.

"There'll be no crying today," Kelly scolded, her cheeks slicked with her own tears.

Laughing, Essence wiped her eyes. "I can't help it. I am so happy for the two of you." She dried her hands on her soft pink maid of honor gown.

"Essence, thank you. Thank you for everything. I owe you and my brother big-time."

"Uh-huh, you just remember that when we need a babysitter," Essence replied, and they shared a laugh.

"You know you can count on me anytime." Kelly

hugged her again and Essence moved over to join her mother and the grandchildren.

As Kelly looked around at the crowd of family and friends, she couldn't remember when she had ever been this happy. Sheyna and Danica were sitting at a small table helping the children eat cake, while Brenna was at the other end, nursing her newborn son, Jabarie Junior.

With her husband on her mind, Kelly looked over to her right, where he stood with the three J's and Mark near the bar. He looked so handsome in his gray tuxedo, she thought. He was laughing at something one cousin had said, but spotted Kelly looking his way. He lowered his drink to the bar, excused himself and closed the distance that separated them.

Kelly's heart pounded as he moved closer. Tears again filled her eyes. She was so thankful to have such a wonderful man in her life. For their wedding they had prepared their own vows, and Diamere's words of love and honor had drawn tears around the room.

As soon as he reached Kelly, Diamere gathered her in his arms and seared her lips with a long, passionate kiss. He slowly pulled back, then gazed down into her eyes lovingly.

"How are you, Mrs. Redmond?"

She loved the way that sounded. "I'm just wonderful, Mr. Redmond."

"Then how about we start saying good-night to our guests then retire?" His words caused a tingling in her chest. Tonight she would be making love to her husband.

"Sounds good to me." They had a suite upstairs for the night, then tomorrow morning they were leaving for a long cruise to Alaska. When she'd planned the trip she didn't care where they went as long as they were together. They figured they would spend much of the eleven-day voyage in bed.

They cut the cake, then danced to a few more songs before saying their goodbyes. Kelly kissed her mother, who was crying, and started crying again herself.

"You take care of my little girl," her mother told Diamere.

"With all my heart," he replied, then kissed her cheek before taking his wife's hand and leading her out of the ballroom and up to the penthouse. The wedding and room had been a gift from the Beaumont family. Diamere and Kelly rode up in the elevator and stopped at the sixteenth floor, which opened right into their luxurious suite.

"Wait a second," Diamere said before Kelly moved another step forward. He scooped his bride into his arms and carried her across the threshold into the elegant cream-and-peach room.

Kelly stared adoringly up at her husband with her arms draped around his neck. "Don't hurt your back."

"Don't worry. Nothing is stopping me from making love to my wife." He pressed his lips to hers, then gently lowered her onto the bed and lay down beside her, pushing her gown to the side. Kelly hadn't thought she could ever feel this much happiness, could ever be this much in love. Diamere completed her.

"I've got something for you," he said as he slid from the bed and moved over to his suitcase, delivered by one of the bellhops earlier. Kelly sat up in bed and waited, her mind burning with curiosity. Diamere came back bearing a small gold box.

"Here, for you," he said as he took a seat beside her. She glanced down at the box and then up at him again. "It's a wedding present."

She opened it to find an exquisite tennis bracelet with diamonds and sapphires. Kelly gasped. "It's beautiful."

"Something beautiful for the most important person in my life."

She held out her arm while he put it around her wrist and secured the clasp. Diamere then pulled her into his arms and kissed her. "I can't wait until we leave tomorrow. I get to have you all to myself for the next eleven days."

Kelly gave her husband a sheepish grin as she said, "I guess we better enjoy it while we can, because in seven months there'll be a new addition to the family."

Diamere grasped her chin and tilted her face so that she was looking up at him. "What did you say?"

Kelly could tell he was holding his breath, hoping he had heard what he thought he had. She knew Diamere wanted children, the more the merrier. He was going to make a wonderful father and she couldn't wait to be a mother. "You heard me. We're going to have a baby."

Diamere jumped from the bed and shouted in happiness. Then, suddenly remembering his beautiful bride, he sank down beside her and cradled her in his arms. "Sweetheart, are you okay? Do you need anything?"

Kelly stared up at her husband with a look of adoration as she shook her head. "Everything I need is right here in front of me." As long as she had him she would never want for anything.

"I love you, Mrs. Redmond," he said as he kissed her again.

A single tear slid from the corner of her eye. "And I love you."

REQUEST YOUR FREE BOOKS!

2 FREE NOVELS
PLUS 2 FREE GIFTS!

KIMANI™
ROMANCE

Love's ultimate destination!

KROM10

Every family has its secrets....

What Mother Never Told Me

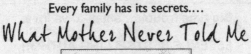

NATIONAL BESTSELLING AUTHOR
DONNA HILL

Raised by her grandmother, Parris McKay finds her life rocked to the core when she discovers the mother she believed dead is still alive. Searching for answers, she heads to France to look for her mother— but locating her opens old wounds for both.

Hurt and disillusioned, Parris finds solace with two new friends who, like Parris, are coming to terms with a legacy of long-buried secrets. And the bond these women forge will sustain them on a journey from heartbreak to healing.

Coming the first week of March 2010 wherever books are sold.